She'd spent yea[rs] through the lens [of] memories and then through that of the media.

An enigmatic, brilliant, ambitious man, who'd then retreated from the world stage, whispered about only as rumors and hearsay.

But Atticus was here now and real, so real. His hands were on her hips, holding her fast, his palms burning through the cotton of the T-shirt she wore. His T-shirt. She'd shivered when she'd put it on and smelled his scent, salt and sun and something deliciously musky and masculine.

Elena shivered again now, surrounded by that same scent, tasting salt as he kissed her, along with a heat that stole her breath. His tongue touched her bottom lip and then pushed inside her mouth, and her head went back, giving him access.

Warmth was beginning to spread through her, a heavy ache gathering between her thighs. She lifted her hands to his chest and spread her fingers out, feeling him, testing his strength beneath the warm cotton of his T-shirt. So hard, like rock.

This was heaven and she wanted more of it.

Jackie Ashenden writes dark, emotional stories with alpha heroes who've just gotten the world to their liking only to have it blown apart by their kick-ass heroines. She lives in Auckland, New Zealand, with her husband, the inimitable Dr. Jax, two kids and two rats. When she's not torturing alpha males and their gutsy heroines, she can be found drinking chocolate martinis, reading anything she can lay her hands on, wasting time on social media or being forced to go mountain biking with her husband. To keep up-to-date with Jackie's new releases and other news, sign up to her newsletter at jackieashenden.com.

Books by Jackie Ashenden

Harlequin Presents

The Innocent's One-Night Proposal
The Maid the Greek Married
His Innocent Unwrapped in Iceland

Rival Billionaire Tycoons

A Diamond for My Forbidden Bride
Stolen for My Spanish Scandal

Three Ruthless Kings

Wed for Their Royal Heir
Her Vow to Be His Desert Queen
Pregnant with Her Royal Boss's Baby

Visit the Author Profile page
at Harlequin.com for more titles.

Jackie Ashenden

A VOW TO REDEEM
THE GREEK

HARLEQUIN
PRESENTS

ISBN-13: 978-1-335-59227-9

A Vow to Redeem the Greek

Harlequin Enterprises ULC
22 Adelaide St. West, 41st Floor
Toronto, Ontario M5H 4E3, Canada
www.Harlequin.com

Printed in U.S.A.

Recycling programs for this product may not exist in your area.

A VOW TO REDEEM
THE GREEK

CHAPTER ONE

ELENA KALATHES SURVEYED the small, un-named Jamaican island in the middle of the Caribbean with some annoyance. All green jungle and white sand beaches, the water a crystal-clear turquoise, it was certainly picturesque. Idyllic almost and untouched. That was what the people in Kingston had told her. Off grid, they said. He has supplies delivered once a month, they said. Sometimes he visits Port Antonio but only rarely and never on a schedule, they said.

No one knows where he lives, they said.

Well, no one apart from the three Kalathes Shipping staff members she'd already sent to Jamaica to find her adoptive brother. And herself.

Not that he was her brother, not in any real sense. She hadn't grown up with him and hadn't seen him since he'd rescued her from the rubble of her home in that tiny Black Sea nation devastated by an earthquake sixteen years ago, bringing her back to the Kalathes Greek island estate, and left her there.

So no, not a brother. A fairy tale, more like. A myth, even.

Atticus Kalathes. Head of the global charity Eleos, and who ran the whole massive enterprise from his off-grid nameless island that he never left. Or only sometimes, though no one could be entirely sure. His movements were a mystery.

The skipper had cut the engine to the boat she'd hired to get to Atticus's island and had leapt out onto the small jetty that stuck out into the clear blue sea. Once the motor died there was no sound apart from the waves lapping against the rocks and the sand, and the occasional cry of seabirds.

Sweat trickled down Elena's spine. Stupid to wear a suit in the tropics, but she'd wanted to present a strong, professional front. She'd thought the lightweight cream jacket wouldn't be too hot considering she was going to be on a boat, and the cream silk blouse she wore underneath would help keep her cool.

A mistake. The sweat was going to stain

the blouse and what had possessed her to wear the matching cream skirt, God only knew.

The heels were a mistake also.

Elena glanced down at the cream kitten heels she'd brought to match her cream suit. Yes, definitely a mistake. She just…well. She liked expensive clothes. She liked to look nice. She was here as Aristeidis Kalathes representative—his adoptive daughter—and it mattered that she look the part.

The skipper tied off the boat and held out a hand to her. Elena took it and gingerly stepped onto the jetty. There were already water stains on her shoes, dammit.

'Thank you,' she said to the skipper. 'Give me an hour.'

He nodded and leapt back into the boat, already getting out the first of what would no doubt be many cigarettes.

Elena turned and glanced down the small jetty then over to the beach beside it, the water lapping gently against the pristine white sand. The heat was punishing, the sun fierce even at this time of the afternoon, and the humidity was making every item of clothing she wore stick uncomfortably to her body.

She hoped an hour would be enough. The

others she'd sent had lasted only ten minutes. Then again, none of them were her. None of them were the little eight-year-old Atticus had rescued from the rubble of a destroyed town, before taking her to Greece and then abandoning her at his childhood home.

She would use that abandonment if she had to. She wasn't above a bit of emotional manipulation, not when it came to fulfilling her adoptive father's dying wish.

Aristeidis wanted to see his son one last time, to heal the breech between them, and Elena would do anything to help him. Aristeidis had given her a home, given her his name, given her security that the traumatised child she'd once been had lost after her entire family had been killed.

He'd given her everything and for the past few years, over the course of his illness, she'd been giving back. Including bringing his estranged son home.

Atticus Kalathes was going to return to Greece, whether he wanted to or not.

She smoothed her skirt, adjusted her jacket, and walked purposely down the wooden jetty. Not far from the beach, crouched beneath the palms and tangled jungle, was a sprawling house constructed of dark wood. It seemed to be a series of boxes connected by wooden walkways, with large floor-to-ceiling windows that looked out over the beach and the ocean.

A sandy path bordered by discreet solar lighting and covered in crushed shells led from the jetty to the house. Elena started along it, only to come to a stop as a movement from the direction of the beach caught her eye.

A man walked across the sand. He'd clearly come from the rocks at the end of the beach and carried something over one muscular, tanned shoulder.

One very bare, muscular, tanned shoulder.

Elena frowned then squinted.

It wasn't just his shoulder that was bare, she realised. He didn't appear to be wearing swimming trunks of any kind.

He was completely naked.

A flush of embarrassed heat washed through her, making the sticky feeling of her clothes even worse, and she looked hurriedly away.

Of course, he would be naked. It was his island. He must think he had complete privacy and yet here she was, charging in unannounced. Well, almost unannounced. She'd sent him numerous emails and voice messages informing him of her visit, none of which he'd responded to, and she'd thought that maybe he hadn't received them. He did live off grid after all.

Or maybe he had received them, he just hadn't wanted to answer. He was famously rude, according to the various Kalathes people who'd tried to make contact with him. Though the people in Kingston had said that the rare times he did venture to the mainland, he was very charming and everyone liked him.

Elena didn't know which version of him she was going to get—she suspected the rude one—but her coming upon him naked wasn't going to endear her. Perhaps she should go back to the boat and wait until he'd got dressed.

She turned towards the jetty and the boat, and took a step.

'Stop,' a deep, masculine voice ordered.

Elena thought of herself as a modern woman, definitely a strong woman, and she didn't take kindly to being told what to do by anyone who wasn't Aristeidis, but she found that she'd obeyed the command before she'd even thought about it.

Annoyed, she turned to tell him that she wasn't a dog to be ordered around, only for the words to die unsaid on her tongue.

Atticus Kalathes stood not far away, bathed in the Caribbean sun like a male version of Botticelli's *Venus*, minus the long blonde hair and the shell.

He was very tall, very broad, and his olive skin was darkly tanned and glistening with water. Every line of him was hard, every muscle exquisitely chiselled as if out of a dark amber marble. His hips were narrow, his legs long, his thighs powerful. And between them...

Elena flushed even deeper and tore her gaze away and up to his face.

But quite frankly that wasn't any better.

She knew what he looked like, of course— Aristeidis had many albums full of photos of a laughing boy with coal-black hair and even blacker eyes. A smiling teenager with hints of the man he'd become in his strong jaw and proud blade of a nose. And she had her own memories, too, of that day so long ago now, when she'd gripped the small pocket-knife she'd found in the rubble of her home, her only weapon as a crowd of looters surrounded her. They'd seen an opportunity in the lone, vulnerable child, armed with only a tiny knife.

She'd been living in the rubble for at least a week, scrounging what food she could find, not wanting to leave the ruins of her apartment building and her family lost somewhere beneath it. She'd been terrified, blood from a cut she hadn't even realised she had running down her face and getting into her eyes. But one thing surviving in the rubble for a week had taught her: the roaming packs of looters were predators and they could sense fear, so if she was caught out in the open, she mustn't ever show she was afraid. Mustn't ever look like prey.

So she'd stood there, fear like acid in her throat even as she'd gripped her knife, trying not to let any of it show. Then *he* had come out of the dark, a tall figure armed to the teeth. He'd worn a helmet and fatigues and he'd lifted his weapon, firing two shots into the air and shouting at the looters in a language she hadn't recognised. The men had scattered and then it was only her and him, and she could see his face, all stark lines and sharply cut angles, and eyes blacker the sky above her head.

A handsome man, she'd thought. A prince maybe. Because he wasn't one of the looters or the opportunists, she'd known that instinctively. He was here to save her, she'd been certain, so she'd dropped her little knife and held out her arms to him.

The eyes that looked at her now were still as black as that long ago sky, as were the uncompromising lines of his face. But she was looking at him now as an adult, not a child, and she could see how beautiful he was. Apollo come down to earth to seduce mortal women.

She'd known that though. She'd seen photos of him in the media, had read avidly all the interviews he'd given. In fact, she knew them all by heart. She could recite them in her sleep. He'd given all of four, the last one two years ago, and hadn't been in the public eye since.

Her heart thumped hard beneath the cream wool and silk of her clothing. The sun glistened in his inky hair, still wet from the swim he'd apparently just had, and there were drops caught in his long, sooty lashes.

She'd seen pictures of naked men before. It wasn't as if she hadn't. In the books in the Kalathes library, photos of paintings and sculptures and other forms of art. She'd peeked, too, on the Internet, looking at various sites out of interest, but she'd privately wondered what all the fuss was about.

Now she knew. Now she understood.

A living, breathing man, glistening in the sunlight, all damp skin, hard muscle, and glittering black eyes. He was the fuss.

He didn't seem the least bit embarrassed or bothered by his nakedness. In fact, he stood there as if he weren't naked at all or carrying some freshly caught fish still attached to a line over his shoulder. He might as well have been wearing a three-piece suit and a crown for all the notice he paid.

She really needed to say something, perhaps the little speech she'd already prepared about how his father was dying and that it was time for him to come home, but the words got jumbled up in her head and all that came out was, 'Um… I…well…'

'You don't have permission to land here,' he said, his deep voice hard.

Elena's mouth had gone dry and her cheeks felt hot. In fact, her whole body felt hot, and it wasn't only the sun or the humidity, she suspected. 'Oh, well, you possibly don't recognise me. I'm—'

'I know who you are, Elena.' He flicked an impersonal glance over her. 'You still don't have permission to land on my island.'

An electric shock went through her and she blinked. He'd recognised her, which she hadn't expected since the last time he'd seen her had been sixteen years ago, when he'd delivered her to Aristeidis and Kalifos, the Greek island where the Kalathes family lived.

She swallowed, reflexively straightening her jacket as if that would make her any cooler. 'I sent you a number of emails, and I called—'

'Yes, and did you at any point get a response from me indicating I would be pleased for a visit?'

It annoyed her that, not only did he not seem to care about his nakedness and its effect on her, he apparently hadn't cared about her emails either. 'No. But I thought they might have gone astray.'

'They did not.'

'But you—'

'My silence should have indicated my preference,' he went on as if she hadn't spoken. 'Which is to be left alone.' Despite the sun gilding his skin, his expression was cold.

It seemed she was going to get rude Atticus Kalathes.

Well, no matter. She was here on a mission for Aristeidis and she wasn't going to let anything get in the way of her goal, not even one beautiful naked man. She was determined if nothing else.

'I'm afraid I can't do that,' she said crisply, pulling herself together. 'I'm here on behalf of your father. He's dying, Atticus. He wants you to come home.'

Atticus had known exactly who the little boat carried when he'd spotted it motoring steadily towards his island not half an hour earlier. He'd been out in the water catching his dinner for the evening and the sight of the boat had put him in a foul temper.

He'd purposefully ignored Elena's emails

and calls because the last thing he wanted was to have to deal with anything related to his father. He'd thought his silence would be enough to deter her. Apparently not.

Honestly, what was the point in living off grid, on an unnamed island that he'd made sure wasn't on any maps, if people could find you so damn easily?

He hadn't bothered with the niceties. If she was so insistent on coming here, to his territory, she could take him as she found him, which was naked, his preferred state on the island when he was catching his own dinner.

She was invading his home and she didn't have an invite, and he'd be damned if he stopped fishing and got dressed to accommodate her.

At least, that was what he'd thought when the boat had pulled up to the jetty at last, and he'd seen her small figure, dressed in an inappropriate cream suit, picking her careful way along the shell path to his door.

Then he'd got a closer look and hadn't been able to think of anything at all.

Sixteen years ago, she'd been a ragged little eight-year-old covered in blood, holding a knife in one small fist against the five men who had certainly meant to do her harm. Her clothes had been torn, her rich blonde hair in braids, her brown eyes full of fury.

He'd been in charge of a private army that helped governments during times of civil unrest or disaster, and had been searching the rubble for survivors. He'd spotted her immediately and the danger she was in, and had sensed that, despite the determination in her posture and the fury in her eyes, she was terrified. As she should have been, considering she was a child surrounded by looters.

He'd fired a couple of warning shots in the air to scatter the men around her, and he'd thought she might run after that because, in fatigues and carrying weapons, he was only likely to frighten her further. Yet she'd taken one look at him, her face bloody from the cut on her forehead, had dropped her knife and held out her little arms to him as if he weren't a hardened mercenary, but her knight in shining armour instead.

He'd never forgotten that. Never forgotten the way his dead heart had given a shudder in his chest at the sight of her.

He hadn't forgotten it now as she stood in front of him, flushed and damp with perspiration in a suit that was more appropriate for the boardroom than the beach of a tropical island.

She'd changed. She'd changed completely.

That rich blonde hair wasn't in braids, but a neat bun on the back of her head, and her face had lost the roundness of childhood. She had a firm chin, a surprisingly lush mouth, a proud nose, and feathery blonde brows a shade lighter than her hair.

That tough, ragged little girl had grown up into a stunningly beautiful woman. A woman who was clearly suffering from the heat and also, he couldn't help but notice, flustered by his nakedness.

That would have made him feel satisfied if she hadn't been who she was, and he hadn't taken a lover in so long he could barely remember the last time he'd touched a woman. His libido was as dead as his heart and he felt no need to resurrect it.

Besides, she wasn't just any woman. She was the girl he'd rescued and left with his father. His father who was dying.

No, he hadn't read any of the emails she'd sent him, but, despite his anger at her arrival, he'd known deep down as soon as he'd seen her boat that if she'd come all this way to find him, it was probably about something serious.

He hadn't spoken to Aristeidis for sixteen years, and had planned on never speaking to him again, yet something unfamiliar stirred deep inside him as soon as the words 'he's dying' were out of her mouth.

Atticus ignored it.

'So?' he asked, a heartless response, which made sense considering he didn't actually have a heart.

Her warm brown eyes narrowed, making it very clear that she didn't approve of his lack of concern. 'What do you mean "so"? You heard what I said, didn't you?'

'That my father is dying and I need to come home? Yes.' He hefted the fish on his shoulder. 'One, I don't care, and two, I'm not going anywhere, so why don't you trot off back to where you came from?'

She blinked in surprise, golden lashes fluttering, and for a moment he thought she might indeed turn on one of her pretty heels and trot off back to the boat. But then those feathery brows arrowed down and that rounded chin got a distinctly determined look to it, and once again he was reminded of that eight-year-old girl, standing in the rubble, facing off five adult men as if she could fight all of them and win.

'No.' Her voice was cool and crisp as a winter frost. 'One, I promised your father I'd bring you home and two, I'm not "trotting" anywhere.'

A pulse of unwelcome electricity arrowed down his spine.

People did not talk back to him. He was head of the largest charity in the world and had a great deal of power and social standing, and he ran Eleos like a military operation. There was a strict hierarchy and he expected his staff to follow orders without question, and they did.

They certainly didn't stand there flushed and sweaty, ignoring a direct command to leave and surveying him with the most intensely disapproving look, as if *he* were in the wrong somehow.

'It was not a request,' Atticus bit out.

She straightened, a stubborn glint igniting in her dark eyes. 'And I'm not one of your employees. I don't have to do what you say.'

'You are, however, on my property. If you don't leave, I'll have you removed.'

She looked around in an exaggerated fashion. 'And who exactly is going to be doing the removing? I don't see anyone else here.'

There was no one else here. He lived alone, which was how he liked it.

'Then I'll remove you myself.' And he went to unhook his fish from over his shoulder as if to put it on the ground in preparation for grabbing her.

It was almost a bluff. Because he'd remove her if he had to. She'd turned up here unwanted and unannounced and so she'd have to deal with the consequences.

She must have believed him though, because her hands came up. 'Wait,' she said in a breathless voice. Perspiration glistened in the soft hollow of her throat and, as he watched, a drop slid slowly down over her skin, following the curve of one full breast. 'I'm not here to fight you.'

For a second he didn't hear her, distracted by that tiny, glistening drop as it slid further down into the shadowed valley of her cleavage, before abruptly realising what he was doing and jerking his gaze back up to her face.

'Then why are you still here?' he demanded. Annoyance had sharpened his voice, but he didn't care. He didn't want her here and a curious heat was running through him. A heat he hadn't felt for a very long time and one he didn't like, not one bit. His body was a machine he kept well oiled and in peak condition, and his command over himself was total. Physical desire was an indulgence and one he didn't permit himself, so he shouldn't be reacting to her like this, not even a flicker.

'I promised him, Atticus,' Elena said firmly. 'I promised him I wouldn't come home without you and so I'm not.'

His father, Aristeidis Kalathes. Head of the Kalathes family. Owner of a multimillion-dollar shipping company. Ex-military. Proud. Arrogant. And rigid as iron.

Aristeidis, a widower left to bring up his two boys after his wife had died far too young, hadn't been any kind of father to Atticus for years, and even when he'd been a child, his father had always been about Dorian, Atticus's beloved older brother.

Dorian who'd died when Atticus was sixteen.

Still grieving his wife, his father had never got over Dorian's death either, and had never forgiven Atticus for being the reason Dorian had died, and Atticus had long since accepted that, because it was true. He *was* the reason Dorian had died, and Aristeidis had been punishing him for it for years.

His father had the right, that was clear. Yet that didn't mean Atticus was going to stay and take it either, so he'd left Kalifos for good. His father had hated him for that too.

No, if Aristeidis wanted him home, it wasn't to reconcile, no matter what he'd told Elena or what she believed herself. Atticus had no doubt the old bastard wanted to punish him some more, in which case he would be destined for disappointment. Atticus had paid for Dorian's death. He'd paid for it a hundred times over, and he was done.

He was never coming home and that was final.

'In that case—' Atticus turned towards his house '—it looks like you'll be in for a long holiday in Jamaica.'

Then he strode past her without another word.

CHAPTER TWO

ELENA STARED AFTER Atticus's taut rear as he disappeared down the shell path and around behind the house, a very real anger coiling tightly in her gut.

Aristeidis had told her that getting Atticus home would be difficult, that their relationship had been broken long ago and it was his own fault. He should have been a better father to Atticus, but he'd let grief and bitterness after Dorian's death drive his only remaining son away.

Now, as the cancer that was killing him made him sicker and sicker, all he wanted was to heal that broken relationship and tell his son how sorry he'd been for the way he'd treated Atticus all these years.

His regret and sadness had only added to the grief that Elena felt herself at his illness, and she couldn't bear the thought that the old man who'd given her a home and a family after she'd lost her own would die without reconciling with his son. She loved Aristeidis. He'd given her so much and it didn't seem like a big thing to bring his son back to him.

She'd thought that the moment she'd told Atticus about his father, he'd want to return. Not that he'd instantly drop everything, of course, but she'd thought he might be upset or at the very least be regretful.

Except he hadn't been. He didn't care, he'd said.

Her anger tightened. True, Aristeidis had made some mistakes after the death of Dorian, but still. He was Atticus's father and he was *dying*. Surely Atticus could put aside his own bitterness for his dying father? Elena didn't remember much about her own father, but she knew she would have done anything to have one last conversation with him.

If you'd managed to get the attention of someone to search through the rubble instead of running and hiding like a coward, you might have had the chance.

Elena ignored the whisper in her head. It was an old doubt that visited from time to time, but she never listened to it. There was no point. She'd been eight when her family had been killed and what could an eight-year-old have done? She'd barely survived herself.

Anyway, getting angry with Atticus wouldn't help the situation. It was a weakness she couldn't afford, and besides, it never got you what you wanted. When Atticus had left her on Kalifos she'd been furious, both at the world and at him. The world for taking away her family and then at him for abandoning her.

Aristeidis had been appalled at her arrival too and hadn't wanted anything to do with an angry child who seemed more spitting, hissing cat than human being. He wasn't a man who approved of strong displays of emotion. He was ex-military and valued strength and control, and so that was what Elena had turned herself into. A strong woman in command of herself and who never let her emotions get the better of her.

She couldn't let those emotions get the better of her now with Atticus. Though…perhaps it wouldn't hurt to let him know how much his father needed him. Perhaps even a small plea. She wouldn't allow herself to be vulnerable, not the way she'd been all those years ago, in the rubble of her devastated town, but she could allow him to think that she was.

She had no idea what kind of man he was now—she hadn't really had any idea of what kind of man he'd been when he'd rescued her all those years ago either—but he was clearly someone who responded to those in need. He ran Eleos, after all, and you didn't start up a charity then turn it into one of the world's biggest without being somewhat of a giver by nature.

Maybe if she was convincing enough he'd change his mind and come home. She'd turn on the tears if she had to. She wasn't above begging, not for Aristeidis's sake.

Taking a steadying breath and forcing her anger away, Elena started off in the direction Atticus had gone. Hopefully when she found him, he'd have put on some clothes, which would help matters.

However, when she eventually found him in a small clearing in the tangled jungle behind the house, standing at a tall wooden bench, he was still naked and in the process of gutting and cleaning the fish he'd caught. He paid her absolutely no attention at all as he stripped the scales from the fish, cut the head and tail off, then deboned it with ruthless efficiency.

And for a second all thoughts of pleading with him vanished from her head as she watched him, half mesmerised by the assured movement of his strong, scarred hands. He looked as if he'd cleaned and filleted his catch a thousand times before, every action precise and confident.

Of course he would. He's a hunter.

Where that thought came from, she had no idea. But it was true, she could see it in the hard, carved muscles of his body and the air of relaxed readiness about him. He didn't take his eyes off the fish he was preparing, but she had the sense that if prey or a threat appeared, he'd grab that knife and attack without hesitation.

'I thought I told you to leave,' he said, casually arrogant as he set aside the fish he'd cleaned and then dealt with the offal without looking up.

The tight coil of anger and grief inside her flexed and even though she was trying not to give into her emotions, what came out was, 'And I thought I told you I wasn't leaving until you came with me.'

'Get back on your boat, Elena. I'm not changing my mind.'

She tore her gaze from the distracting motion of his hands. 'Why not?'

'I'm not explaining myself either.' He looked up all of a sudden, his gaze black and glittering, the wickedly sharp boning knife held loosely in his hand. 'Make no mistake. I will forcibly remove you if I have to.'

An inexplicable shiver worked its way down her spine. Still naked, tanned by the sun, and holding a knife, there was something wild about him, something primal and, really, she should have been afraid of him.

Yet despite her anger, she found herself strangely thrilled instead.

Over the years she'd built up this idea of him, the warrior who'd saved her, the prince who'd carried her to safety. He was a fairy tale she'd embellished in her head and how could she not? At first Aristeidis had never spoken of him, not when she was growing up, that didn't happen until she'd been in her teens, so she'd had nothing real to base her imaginings on. Nothing but his rise as head of Eleos and she'd only watched that the way everyone else had—through the eyes of the media.

But this man in front of her wasn't a fairy tale and he wasn't a prince. He wasn't a myth. He was real and the reality of him was covered in scales and fish blood and holding a knife, and she found that oddly exciting, though why, she didn't know.

She wasn't leaving, though, regardless of his threats.

'Please, Atticus.' She let a thread of grief colour her voice and she didn't have to fake it. 'He hasn't even got a month. He needs you.'

'No,' he said, very obviously unmoved.

Elena clasped her hands in front of her and twisted them, making her eyes large and dark, and pouting just enough to hint at tears rather than a sulk. 'He's your father. It would mean so much to him.' She paused. 'It would mean so much to me too.'

While the hints at vulnerability were fake, she wasn't lying. It *would* mean so much to Aristeidis and it would mean so much to her as well. She wanted him and his father to reconcile, for both their sakes.

But he was already turning away, her little performance of no interest to him. 'I've already told you my decision. I'd go now if I were you. There will be a storm front blowing in at some point this evening.'

Frustration gripped her, but she knew better than to give in to it.

You were too impatient. You should have waited for him to invite you here.

Except he was clearly never going to. No, what she needed was a bit more time and a better moment to broach the topic. Rushing him into this while he was catching and preparing his dinner, and then insisting when he was already in a bad temper, had been foolish.

Certainly the way she'd learned to endear herself to Aristeidis in those first few difficult months after she'd arrived on Kalifos was to approach him when he was in a good mood, after he'd just had a delicious meal or after a long sleep. Or in the evenings as he relaxed in the salon with his favourite brandy.

She'd kept her grief and her fear, her anger and her pain buried, letting not a hint of them show, sitting beside him quietly like a good little girl instead. And eventually, after a week of silence and her learning as much

Greek as she could, he'd asked her what her name was.

He hadn't ignored her after that. He'd needed someone to take care of, she'd gradually realised, and, since she'd needed someone to take care of her, she'd turned herself into his perfect daughter.

Not that she was going to do that for Atticus, but perhaps a little neediness wouldn't go astray in the right context. First, though, she needed to give him time to finish preparing his fish, get dressed, and maybe when he was done he'd be more amenable. Especially if she got rid of her means of transport to the island. He could hardly put her on a boat back to the mainland if there wasn't a boat to put her on. And if there was a storm front coming, he wouldn't be able to take her back in any boat he might have either.

'Fine,' she said quietly. 'I'll go.' Without waiting for his response, she turned and strode off in the direction of the jetty. The skipper was sitting in the boat, casually smoking, and when Elena told him that she wasn't going to need his services for a return trip after all, he nodded and began the business of untying the boat.

It was a risk she was taking and she had no idea what Atticus was going to do when he found she'd sent her ride back to Kingston away, but it would buy her some time, that was for certain.

How she was going to convince him to return to Greece, she still had no idea, but somehow she'd find a way. She'd drag him back kicking and screaming if she had to. Though given he was at least six four and she was five two that probably wasn't going to work, but still.

Aristeidis wanted him home and she'd do anything for Aristeidis.

Elena waited until the boat had left and was on its way back to Port Antonio, then she waited a bit, giving Atticus some time to finish with his stupid fish and get some clothes on. He'd no doubt see the boat and think she was on her way back, so wouldn't be best pleased to find out she wasn't.

But that was too bad. She had a stubborn streak a mile wide and she had a sense she might need it when it came to him. In fact, she had a sense that he might equal her in stubbornness.

That should have made her wary, but it

didn't. For some reason it excited her instead, which was worrying. She didn't want to be excited by him. While he was beautiful, his attitude towards his dying father—however Aristeidis had earned it in the past—still left a lot to be desired and she did not like that, not one bit.

After she'd waited what she hoped was a sufficient amount of time, she set off purposefully down the shell path again, following it back around the side of the house to the clearing and the bench where he'd cut up his fish.

Atticus wasn't there.

The path led on, however, wending through palms and shrubs, and around another of the boxes connected by glass corridors that were part of the house, following on to the beach.

She went along it until she was almost at the beach and then she saw him, standing under an outdoor shower situated beneath a shady palm.

Her mouth dried.

The water cascaded down over him, outlining the hard ridges of every cut muscle, his body honed to perfection, his olive skin tanned and smooth, with a sprinkle of dark hair over his chest and following down his sculptured stomach and then further down...

She swallowed, but this time she couldn't stop herself from staring.

He was beautiful. He was beautiful everywhere. She almost couldn't believe he was real.

He stood for a moment, outlined in sun and water, then, obviously becoming aware of her, he shut the shower off, his black gaze colliding with hers, unmistakable anger lighting in it. His expression hardened.

Elena felt something in her harden too. Well, she knew he wouldn't be happy, but that didn't mean she'd let him intimidate her. In the first couple of months of being on Kalifos, Aristeidis would sometimes go into black moods, which were frightening. But she'd survived an earthquake that had killed everyone in her town, lived for a week on her own, facing off against looters, before being dumped on a Greek island in the care of a complete stranger. She was a survivor and she wasn't going to let one old man scare her. So she hadn't. And he'd respected her for it.

She suspected, however, that Atticus wouldn't, so she let her eyes get all big and dark and wounded, spreading her hands in a helpless gesture. 'I'm sorry, the boat wasn't there. Seemed the captain got tired of waiting and took off.' She fluttered her eyelashes, trying to be a bit pathetic. 'I'm so sorry, but… Well. It looks like I'm stuck here.'

Atticus didn't move for one long endless moment, his magnificent body gleaming like dark amber in the sun. Then abruptly he started towards her, intent in every line of him.

Alarm arrowed down her spine, all her threat senses going on high alert.

'What are you doing?' she asked, dropping the pathetic act instantly.

He didn't answer, striding towards her, the expression on his face utterly unreadable. But there was no mistaking the anger in his eyes.

Elena took a step back, her alarm increasing. 'Wait,' she began, except by then it was much too late. He took one last step and then she was swept up into his arms, his wet skin soaking her lovely cream suit.

'Atticus, what are you doing?' she repeated, too shocked to even struggle.

'I told you what would happen if you didn't leave,' he said in a hard voice.

Her heart was thumping, her pulse wild. 'Let me go,' she demanded hoarsely.

But he didn't answer, striding with her in his arms over the glittering white sand, heading towards the deep turquoise of the water.

If she hadn't been so shocked, she might have been conscious of the heat of his skin and the strength of him, and how she'd never been in the arms of a naked man before. But she was shocked and she had no time to think of those things, because then he was wading into the sea.

Every muscle in her body tightened. Oh, no, he wasn't going to do what she thought he was going to do… Was he?

'There,' he said. 'You can swim home.'

Then he unceremoniously dumped her into the ocean.

Atticus never let his temper get the better of him. He never let *any* emotion get the better of him. He'd successfully managed to detach himself from anything resembling feelings for years, firstly by joining the military in an effort to appease his father not long after Dorian's death, where he'd constantly challenged himself physically, pushing for perfection until he'd reached the peak as an elite sniper. Then once that had been achieved and it was clear that even following in his father's footsteps wouldn't heal Aristeidis's hatred of him, he'd continued his military career, assembling a private army that sold their services to governments who needed help with security concerns, peacekeeping, disaster relief, and protection for its citizens.

That might have been enough for him if he hadn't found Elena in the rubble of her town, prompting old feelings to re-emerge, and so he'd had to reassess his career yet again. He'd been independently wealthy by then, and had decided to put his military planning skills into starting a charity, and had been so successful that Eleos had become a worldwide phenomenon almost before he knew it.

Success and recognition had followed on its heels, and that should have satisfied him. Yet it hadn't. He'd been conscious instead of a growing realisation of all the things that he had that Dorian didn't. Fame. Money. Power. A life he had that Dorian didn't.

It wasn't fair and it wasn't right, not when he was the reason Dorian was dead, and he

soon found he'd lost his taste for the spot-
light—not that he'd ever really had it in the
first place. Part of him had wanted to give
Eleos up, but his name was now inextrica-
bly linked with it and he hadn't wanted to do
anything to jeopardise its success. So he'd
retreated to his Jamaican island and the simple life he'd found for himself there, running
Eleos from his office and putting in the occasional appearance when it was demanded
of him, for the good of the charity.

But the fact was, he needed the island and
its simplicity, where he needed to exist only
in the moment. Where he could concentrate
on making sure he stayed as detached as he
could from the past.

Then Elena had turned up.

Elena, bringing with her everything he'd
thought he'd put behind him. Elena, all
dressed in white, reminding him of the small
blonde warrior with blood on her face and a
knife clutched in her hand. Elena, not a child
any longer...

He'd wanted her gone and out of his life,
and he'd thought, when she'd walked away
just before, that she'd obeyed his command
and left him to it. He'd even felt satisfied

when he'd heard the roar of the boat's engine, and had ignored that odd twist of what surely couldn't have been regret.

So he'd gone and showered off the remains of the fish blood and scales, only for Elena to suddenly reappear, looking at him with big dark eyes and spreading her hands helplessly, telling him the captain of the boat had just left without her.

The last time he'd seen Elena had been on Kalifos, where he'd handed her over to the Kalathes' housekeeper, Sofia, telling her that Elena was an orphan and that she was going to be living with them from now on.

Elena's brown eyes had been full of hot anger that day and as he'd handed her over into Sofia's care, she'd looked at him with complete and utter betrayal. She hadn't wanted to stay on Kalifos, she'd wanted to stay with him. And that was impossible. He was a soldier, he couldn't take care of an eight-year-old girl. Especially not a fiery, stubborn, tough eight-year-old who'd argued with him the whole long journey from her ruined country back to Athens and then to Kalifos.

A fiery, stubborn eight-year-old girl whom

he suspected was just as fiery and stubborn as a woman, and not at all the helpless maiden she made out. Maybe it was that which had ignited his own anger. Or maybe it was simply because in that ridiculous white suit she was beautiful and the thought of her being in his vicinity and waking up a libido he'd thought long dead was insupportable.

His detachment had already been compromised by her mere presence, and when he'd realised she hadn't left with the boat and had actually come back, he'd noticed her watching him, a familiar look on her face. He knew that look. It was the look of a woman who liked what she saw and she liked what she saw in him.

The male animal in him didn't care who she'd once been to him. It didn't care that she was associated with a past he'd been trying for nearly twenty years to leave behind. All it knew was that she was beautiful and it had been so long since he'd had a woman, and so his temper had frayed and his patience along with it.

He'd had to do something to teach her a lesson in obedience, so he'd shut off the shower and come towards her, ignoring the alarm on her face as he'd swept her into his arms. Then he'd turned in the direction of the sea and continued across the sand.

A mistake, and he'd realised it the moment he'd touched her. She was warm in his arms—hot even—and so soft, and it had been a long time since he'd felt a woman's curves against him. She'd made a breathless little sound and her scent had been all delicate musk and the crisp bite of apples, so sweet. He couldn't remember how long it had been since he'd experienced sweetness, or soft heat and honeyed skin.

She'd wriggled against him as he'd waded out into the water, the movement of her body exciting him. He'd wanted to hold her closer, bury his face in her neck and inhale her scent, and abruptly his control had felt tenuous.

So he'd dropped her straight into the water.

It wasn't deep, only waist height for him, but when she gave a startled cry and went under, there was a second where he felt a brief alarm, wondering if she could swim and whether he'd have to rescue her. But then she found her feet and stood up, water streaming off her.

And his mistake was compounded. Be-

cause her clothing was soaked and mould-
ing to her curves, and her white silk blouse
had gone completely transparent. He could
see the delicate lace of the white bra she wore
beneath it, and the soft shell-pink of little nip-
ples gone hard in the cool of the sea.

She didn't look helpless or wounded now.
Now, she looked furious, virtually quivering
with rage. She spat a filthy curse at him in
Greek and then her palm flashed out and she
hit the water, sending up a splash that caught
him full in the face.

The male animal in him growled in anger,
wanting to close the distance between them
and take hold of her. Perhaps dump her back
in the water again or maybe something better, such as stripping off her wet clothes so
she was as naked as he was, then pressing all
that silky skin against him. Take her mouth,
taste the salt on her lips.

His detachment, his control, wavered, and
there was a moment where he had to fight to
keep his grip on it. No, he couldn't do that.
He'd *never* do that, not with her. Not only
was she still that little girl to him, she was
also now his adoptive sister and nothing was
going to happen between them. If he wanted

sex so badly, he'd make a trip into Port Antonio later and find a willing woman there. It didn't have to be her.

Instead, he wiped the water from his face and turned, wading out of the sea without a word, heading towards the house.

He needed to get himself under control, get dressed, and then figure out just what the hell he was going to do with her. Because he hadn't lied when he'd told her about the storm front coming. Although the weather was perfect now, it wouldn't be for long, and there was no time to get his own boat out and take her back to the mainland.

'Atticus!' Elena shouted after him from the water, still sounding furious. 'Why did you do that? Where are you going?'

'There's a towel beside the shower,' he called back, without turning around. 'Leave your wet clothes there and once you've washed yourself off, come into the house.'

'What?' He could hear splashing behind him. 'Atticus, wait!'

But he didn't wait, striding across the hot sand and into the cool shade of the palms. He needed to get away from her and find his control again.

Inside, his house was beautifully cool—as he'd designed it to be—and the smooth dark wood of the floors was soothing after the hot sand. The ceilings were high, with exposed beams, the walls plain white. The living area featured large, louvred doors opened onto a wide deck that overlooked the lagoon. Today he had all the doors open, sunlight flooding in.

The peace and the familiarity of his home settled his frayed temper somewhat, and by the time he walked down the glass-walled corridor that led from the main living area and kitchen of the house down to another, smaller structure that was his bedroom and bathroom, he was feeling calmer.

Rinsing off in the shower, he then pulled on some clothes—worn jeans and a black T-shirt. The same louvred doors were in the bedroom too and they were also standing open, letting in the sun from the beach. He could see the outdoor shower from where he stood and Elena approaching and staring at it before glancing towards the house.

He turned away. She hadn't bothered with his privacy, but he would give her hers. God knew he didn't need any more temptation anyway.

On his way back to the living area, he made a detour down another glass-walled hallway that led to his office. It faced the jungle and the doors in this room opened onto a cool, shady deck. This was his head of operations, where he ran Eleos. There were computer screens and bookcases, one desk to work at, another that functioned as a workbench where he fixed electronics and anything else that needed fixing. Living on the ocean where the salt got into everything, there was always something that needed to be repaired.

He ran as much as he could off solar power, but he did have a back-up generator, his Internet coming from a satellite link.

Reflexively he checked the screens that were streaming news channels and social media to see if anything was happening globally that he needed to know about, but all was as usual so he directed his attention to the most reliable weather site.

The storm front would hit in about an hour, not enough time for him to get rid of Elena, and it was slow moving too, which meant she'd likely have to stay the night.

He bit off a curse. Perhaps he should just get the boat out and take her anyway. He could navigate through a storm. He'd done it before. Then again, he didn't want to risk her, and besides, why was he allowing himself to get so hot under the collar about her? She was a pretty woman, but he'd been around pretty women before without getting so wound up. And why did it matter that she stayed? He'd already told her he wasn't going back to Greece and he certainly wanted nothing whatsoever to do with his father, dying or not.

Are you sure about that?

He ignored the tug of doubt. Of course he was sure. The old man had burned so many bridges there was nothing left of them, not even a structure, and Atticus had no interest in building more.

Elena had been the last bridge he'd tried to build. She'd been an atonement of sorts for Dorian's death, not a replacement but a second chance. She'd also been something of a goodbye, since he hadn't been back to Greece since.

He'd checked in every so often with Kalathes staff to see how she was getting on, that his father was looking after her and that she was happy. And indeed, the reports had all come back that Elena was thriving on Kalifos, getting a decent education and Aristeidis was taking an interest in her.

He'd been satisfied, pleased that the girl he'd rescued was finding happiness somehow. Then word had come a few years later that Aristeidis would be formally adopting her, and he'd been surprised by the jolt that had given him. It hadn't been pain precisely, but he'd decided he wasn't interested in finding out exactly what it was or why, so he'd ignored it.

Elena was safe and now she had a family and that was all that mattered.

It was all that mattered still.

She could stay, it wouldn't be a problem. If she kept going on about his father then he'd just tell her the subject was done and he wasn't interested in hearing any more.

His temper easing now he had a plan, Atticus turned from his screen.

He had a guest bedroom. She could sleep

there and then he'd send her on her way come
morning.

She wouldn't get under his skin any more
than she already had.

He wouldn't let her.

CHAPTER THREE

ELENA GLANCED ONCE again towards the house then, muttering curses under her breath, she began to peel off her wet clothes.

She was furious, utterly and completely furious.

How dared he dump her in the sea? There had been absolutely no call for that kind of behaviour, none at all, and now her lovely new suit and silk blouse were ruined. She'd also lost both shoes, as well as a good portion of her dignity.

You've only got yourself to blame. He'd warned you.

Yes, he had. But she'd thought he'd settle for shouting at her. She hadn't thought he'd actually lay hands on her and throw her in the water.

A shiver ran through her at the memory of those strong, scarred hands holding her, and the heat of his skin as she'd lain briefly against his chest. He'd been so hard too; it had been like lying on sun-warmed rock.

Then had come the cold shock of the water—cold in comparison to him, at least—and the sudden surge of anger that had accompanied it. At him for not listening to her and not caring about his father, and then having the temerity to toss her into the ocean with no care for her clothes or her person. He could at least have explained his issues. He didn't have to resort to childish games.

Still, it was ridiculous to be *quite* so angry at him. She did have a quick temper, it was true, but she'd spent years keeping it in check. She shouldn't have lost it over an unexpected dunking, splashing him like a little kid. She should have been calmer, more controlled, not let him get to her.

Shivering as she pushed down her skirt and kicked it off, she glanced once again towards the house, debating whether or not to take off her wet underwear as well. But while he might be comfortable walking around naked, she wasn't, so she decided to keep it on.

She turned the shower on and stepped under the water. It was lukewarm and in other circumstances she would have enjoyed the cool feel of the water over her hot skin, but she was still too angry to enjoy it.

Keeping the shower short, she rinsed off the sea water then picked up the white fluffy towel that sat on a rock nearby and dried herself. Half the pins had come out of her bun so she took the rest out and squeezed the water from her hair, before wrapping the towel firmly around herself and making her way back along the shell path to the house.

Most of one wall of the house consisted of huge louvred doors that stood open onto a large wooden deck, so she went in a little hesitantly, finding herself in a cool room with a high ceiling of exposed beams and a few skylights. A couple of low couches and squishy, comfortable-looking chairs were scattered about, a big, brightly coloured rug covering the polished wood of the floor. A low coffee table carved out of dark wood stood near the couches, the surface cluttered with books and magazines.

There were shelves against the walls, full of books and shells and pieces of driftwood, and sea glass, as well as a few small hand-carved wooden sculptures. It felt low-key and casual and very comfortable with the sunlight dappling the floor and the warm, salty breeze coming in from the ocean.

A peaceful place. She could see why he liked it.

Until you invaded it.

Well, she wasn't going to apologise for that. His father was dying and wanted him home, and he hadn't even bothered to have a proper conversation with her. And she wasn't leaving until he had.

The living area was empty so she went through another doorway and into a large, airy hallway. There were a couple of other doorways that led off it, down the glass-walled corridors she'd seen from the outside. She peered cautiously down them but didn't see anyone, so she walked along a bit until the hallway opened up on one side to reveal a kitchen and dining area separated by a long wooden bench top.

Atticus was standing at the bench preparing what looked like a marinade for the fish that he'd put in a metal bowl.

So. Not only had he caught his own fish, he was now preparing it and would no doubt cook it too.

It shouldn't have surprised her—despite the money he'd earned from the private army he'd once owned, he was famous for his simple living, eschewing the usual trappings of wealth. He had no cars or planes. No houses in every country. He kept no personal staff. He attended no parties or galas or nightclubs or, indeed, any social occasions. He gave no interviews these days and sought no attention, which of course made everyone even more curious about him.

Yet despite all of that, she was still surprised. In her head he'd become this mythic being, not a man doing something as mundane as preparing a marinade with casual efficiency and who was, at last, mercifully wearing jeans and a T-shirt. He looked far too good in them, as attractive in simple cotton as he was in nothing but his own skin.

He didn't look up. 'I'll deal with your wet things. The second hallway on the left leads to a guest bedroom and I've put some fresh clothes on the bed for you. The storm will be here in less than an hour and it's slow moving so you won't be going anywhere tonight. I'll run you back to Port Antonio tomorrow.'

Elena opened her mouth to thank him, but

he went on before she could speak, 'Also, I will not be entering into any discussion about my father or returning to Greece, and if you bring the subject up, you'll find yourself having it on your own.' Finally he glanced up, a brief glittering flash of obsidian. 'I hope you like fish. Because that's what's for dinner.'

There was an instant where she couldn't have said whether she liked fish or not, because that brief moment of eye contact had short-circuited her brain. She swallowed, trying to pull herself together. She had no idea what was happening to her, but whatever it was, she didn't like it. Her experience of men was exceedingly limited, it was true, and that had been deliberate. Caring for Aristeidis since he'd got sick and helping him with Kalathes Shipping was far more important to her than sex and, anyway, she hadn't met anyone she'd been interested in.

Until now.

Elena ignored the thought. Atticus might be far more attractive than he had any right to be, but she wasn't going to allow herself to get distracted, not when Aristeidis was relying on her to bring him home.

'What do you mean you won't be entering

into any discussion?' she asked. 'Your father is dying, Atticus.'

'Yes. You've told me so three times already.'

'But…doesn't that mean anything to you?'

He didn't look up from his marinade. 'What did I say about this conversation?'

Elena wanted to tell him what he could do with his arrogant pronouncements and almost did so, but there was no doubting the warning in his voice, so she bit down on the hot words she wanted to say. Again, she had to control her temper. If she pushed, he'd remove himself from the conversation and that wouldn't be in Aristeidis's best interest or hers. No, she had to play along for now. She'd figure out a way to get through to him, and at least, from what he'd said about the storm, she had a whole night to try to convince him.

Maybe she could even find out exactly why, even after all the time that had passed, he was still so angry with his father, and why returning to Greece was so out of the question.

'Fine,' she said, quelling her impatience. 'Yes, I like fish.' She was tempted to add that she'd often had it on Kalifos, but decided that would be too pointed. 'Thank you for cooking for me.'

Again, he glanced at her, his black gaze oddly searing. 'I'm not cooking for you, Elenitsa. You just happen to be here while I'm cooking.'

Elenitsa.

What he'd called her all those years ago, after he'd rescued her and she'd told him her name. After he'd discovered that she was all alone, that everyone she knew and everyone she'd loved had died in the earthquake. That she'd been surviving for a week on her own, with no one and nothing.

She hadn't known Greek or English, but he'd had a smattering of the Russian that was her birth language, and so he'd taught her a few words of both so they could communicate. He'd told her that he would take her away and find her a family, but all she'd wanted then was to stay with him. He was her saviour, her protector. He'd cared for her when no one else had and she didn't want or need anyone else.

Abruptly, she didn't want him to call her Elenitsa. He'd abandoned her; he didn't have a right to it. Only Aristeidis did.

'Don't call me that,' she snapped, her temper already on a short leash. 'Only your father gets to call me that.'

Atticus looked up, something gleaming in his gaze. 'How quickly you forget who saved you all those years ago. And it was not my father.'

A strange, hot thrill chased along her skin and she found herself lifting her chin in response, as if he'd challenged her. 'And how quickly you forget who you abandoned all those years ago. Who you left alone in a foreign country, with complete strangers.'

He didn't look away. 'I did not forget. Are we going to have the same argument now as we did back then? When you were eight years old?'

She felt a flush creep over her cheeks. She didn't want him reminding her of the child she'd once been, and she didn't want him treating her like that either. The angry, abandoned child who'd been left by everyone who'd cared about her. The needy, desperate child...

Well, she wasn't that child any more. She wasn't needy or desperate or vulnerable in any way. Aristeidis loved her and had told her that he'd made provision for her in his will so she wouldn't be left with nothing after his death. It mattered to him that she was looked after once he was gone.

From out of nowhere came a sudden surge of the grief that had become her constant companion since Aristeidis's health had declined. It was nice that he'd thought of her, but money was a poor substitute for a person. He was her only family and once he was gone, she'd have no one.

Again.

The grief must have showed on her face because Atticus frowned abruptly, his gaze sharpening. 'What is it?' he asked.

But she wasn't going to explain her grief, not to him, not when it was still too close to the surface. It made her feel too vulnerable and she couldn't bear the thought of being vulnerable in front of this hard, uncompromising man. The man who'd once praised her bravery and strength, making her feel as if she was indeed brave and strong and not just a coward who'd run and hid instead of getting help for her family.

Grief wrapped its cold fingers around her throat, squeezing tighter.

Elena turned away, clutching her towel around her. 'I'm going to get changed,' she muttered and fled.

Atticus watched Elena's small figure disappear back down the hallway and frowned. For a second there she'd looked almost distraught and he couldn't think what he'd said to upset her. He'd only mentioned the argument they'd had when she'd been a child and he'd left her on Kalifos, but that had been years ago. Surely she couldn't still be angry about that? She was an adult now and should understand why he hadn't been able to take her with him.

Or perhaps leaving a traumatised child in the company of complete strangers wasn't such a great idea after all?

Doubt tugged at him again, but he pushed it aside and looked back down at the marinade he was preparing.

What else could he have done? He'd been twenty-three, a mercenary soldier growing his small private army, and there had been no way he could have looked after a child. Not that he could have even if he'd wanted to. He would never be father material and

he'd already had ample proof that he wasn't
big brother material either. On Kalifos she'd
wanted for nothing. So why would she still
be angry that he'd left her alone? If that was
even what she was upset about.

*Why are you so curious? Does it matter
why?*

He didn't know and it didn't matter. She
wasn't his responsibility and hadn't been for
some time, and, apart from anything else, she
was an adult now. Her reasons were her own
and they were none of his business.

Irritated with himself for even bothering to
think about it, Atticus concentrated on finish-
ing up the marinade, putting his fish into it,
then putting the bowl into the fridge.

Yet his thoughts kept straying back to
Elena and how she'd looked wrapped up in
that white towel, with her blonde hair hang-
ing damply over her shoulders and curling
as it dried. She'd clearly kept her underwear
on since he'd seen the delicate straps of her
bra, and that beast in him had wanted to pull
her towel away, pull that bra away too so that
nothing marred the smooth perfection of her
skin.

It had liked her snapping at him when he'd

called her Elenitsa, as well, and then when she'd lifted her chin, responding to his challenge about their old argument. There had been electricity in the air between them, he'd felt it, and he was pretty sure she'd been aware of it too, though maybe she hadn't known what it meant.

Again, though, that was something he shouldn't be thinking about, most definitely not.

Even more irritated at himself and the direction of his thoughts, Atticus busied himself with getting her wet clothing. He rinsed her skirt, jacket and blouse, and hung them out to dry in a covered area near the house, though he was pretty certain the items were ruined, in which case he'd buy her some replacements.

After he'd finished dealing with that, he went back into the living area to find Elena standing in front of one of the shelves and looking at the items on it.

The only clothing he had in the house was his, so he'd found an old white T-shirt and a pair of loose, linen drawstring trousers that would have fitted her. Except all she wore now was the T-shirt, which hung down almost to her knees, leaving a pair of shapely calves and ankles bare.

It made something twist hard inside him, something hot and almost...possessive. As if he liked seeing her wearing nothing but a T-shirt. *His* T-shirt.

'What happened to the trousers?' The words came out more like a demand than a question, but he didn't bother to temper it.

She glanced at him then down at her bare legs. 'I had to roll them up so much it was ridiculous. The T-shirt is fine.'

The T-shirt was *not* fine. It left far too much of her bare skin on show, though why he should even find that troubling, he had no idea.

His control over himself and his environment was perfect, so he had no excuse for getting hot and bothered over the potential glimpse of one pretty woman's thighs. Certainly not enough to get her to change.

'You'll have to wear them tomorrow when I take you back,' he said shortly. 'I've hung your other clothes out, but they're unlikely to be dry by morning, not in this humidity or with the storm coming. I'll have to buy you some replacements.'

She'd turned back to the shelf, studying a small wooden sculpture of a rearing horse. 'Yes, please. Considering you were the one who dumped me in the sea without warning.'

'I gave you plenty of warning.'

'Not that you were going to make me swim back to my boat.'

'If you'd actually left with your boat instead of coming back to lie about it, then I wouldn't have made you swim back to it.'

She glanced at him again, her brown eyes glittering with anger. 'They said you were rude. I had no idea just *how* rude.'

Perhaps that should have made him feel ashamed or at least a little bit embarrassed. It did not. Most people knew that coming to his island unannounced would ensure an unpleasant reception and he didn't apologise for it.

'If you'd wanted a different reception then perhaps you should have waited for an invitation,' he said coldly.

'If you don't want people to turn up unannounced then perhaps you should try replying to your emails,' she snapped back.

Theos, the woman was impossible. She'd been tough, he remembered that, but had she always been such a little spitfire? And how had his father handled that? Aristeidis had been stern and quite the disciplinarian and hadn't put up with what he'd termed 'nonsense'. Surely he wouldn't have been so indulgent of her? How could he? When he'd cut Atticus off so completely after Dorian's death?

Perhaps he mellowed?

No, he shouldn't even be thinking about his father. Yet another reason why Elena's presence here was an irritant that he needed to get rid of as soon as possible.

Except you like her being an irritant. You like fighting with her.

He did not. It was a mistake and if she couldn't keep control of her temper then it was up to him to stay in control of his own, no matter how much she annoyed him.

'Peace, Elena,' he said. 'You're here for the night so let's not make it any more unpleasant than it already is.'

She bristled and looked as if she might snap at him again, then her lush mouth compressed and she turned back to the shelf again. 'I like this horse,' she said after a moment. 'Where did you get it?'

Trying to relax his tight muscles, Atticus thrust his hands into his pockets. 'I didn't get it anywhere. I made it.'

Her brown eyes went wide and she glanced at him again. 'You did?'

'Yes. Carving occupies my hands and I find it relaxing.'

She reached out and touched the horse's head with a delicate finger. Her nails were short and painted the same kind of shell pink as he'd glimpsed through her bra in the sea, and for some reason the way she touched the sculpture sent a bolt of heat through him. 'It's beautiful.'

The bolt of heat intensified, though he wasn't sure why. He didn't need her praise. He carved because it focused him and, as he'd said, relaxed him. He didn't do it for any other reason and he wanted to tell her that, but he was trying to control his raw temper, so all he said was, 'Thank you.'

Elena stared at the horse a moment longer then she turned around and stared at him, her gaze very direct. 'Look, I know you said you didn't want to talk about your father, but I—'

'No,' he interrupted flatly. 'I told you we would not be having this discussion.'

'But—'

'No,' he repeated, and turned to the doorway. He'd told her he wasn't going to talk about this and he'd meant it He'd made his decision and there would be no changing it.

Are you sure? Do you really want to leave things as they are?

He absolutely could. The old man had never cared to talk to him before Aristeidis found out he was dying, so why should Atticus be the one to make the effort now? Did his father really want to mend things between them or was it only the prospect of having a clean soul before he faced his heavenly reckoning?

Either way, Atticus wasn't going to help him.

He started for the doorway to the hall, but found that Elena had nipped past him and was now standing directly in his way.

She wasn't very tall—the top of her head only came up to his chest—and she seemed delicate, especially wearing his T-shirt. However, determination radiated from her and there was a stubborn look in her deep brown eyes.

'No,' she said. '*You* listen to me, Atticus. We will be having this decision and we'll be having it now. I want to know why you won't come home. Why you're insisting on putting what you want ahead of your dying father's wishes.'

He ignored her, sidestepping and intending to go around her, but she sidestepped too, again in his way. 'Have a conversation with me,' she insisted. 'Give me something I can tell Aristeidis.'

His patience frayed, the threads on it snapping one by one as once again he tried to go around her. Again she blocked him. 'You can try and avoid me all you want. But I'm not going to let you.'

'Get out of the way,' he ordered through gritted teeth. 'If you continue to be a nuisance, I'll put you on that boat and the storm be damned.'

She gave him the most dismissive look. 'Don't be childish. Give me one good reason why you don't want to come home. I think you owe me that at least.'

And just like that his temper snapped completely.

He was tired of her being here, reminding him of the past. Reminding him of all the painful things he'd put behind him. Reminding him that he still had a heart whether he liked it or not, and that he still felt things even though he didn't want to. Reminding him that his body was hungry for a woman's touch and that she was beautiful, and he didn't like that. Not at all.

'I *owe* you?' he demanded, closing the gap between them, getting close to her, looming over her. 'I owe you for what? I rescued you. I gave you a home. I gave you a family. I gave you a future. I owe you *nothing*.'

Another woman might have found him intimidating and backed away. But not Elena. She didn't give an inch, staring straight up at him as if he weren't taller than she was and much bigger, much stronger. 'You left me alone in a country I didn't know, in the care of man who was a stranger to me, who didn't speak my language and didn't want a child dumped on him.' Bright golden sparks of anger glittered deep in the warm brown of her eyes. 'And this was *after* I'd lost everything and everyone I'd ever loved. So yes...' She lifted a finger and jabbed him hard in the chest. 'You *do* owe me.'

He didn't know what came over him in that moment, a sudden rush of fury and, beneath it, a flood of pain he hadn't realised he still felt, and he raised his hands so he could lift her and put her out of his way. Or at least that was what he intended.

Yet the moment his hands settled on her hips, all he could feel was the heat of her body beneath the T-shirt, and how seductive it was. How lush her sulky mouth looked and how he could think of a much better way to get her to be quiet.

'Atticus,' she said, her feathery blonde brows descending. 'What are you doing? We need to talk about—'

But she never got to tell him what it was they needed to talk about, because by that stage Atticus had got tired of listening too.

If she wouldn't get out of his way or be quiet, then he'd do something else to silence her.

He bent his head and covered her mouth with his.

CHAPTER FOUR

ELENA KNEW WHAT he was going to do—the flare of heat in his eyes had been warning enough. Not that she needed it, given the electricity in the air that had surrounded them just before his hands had settled on her hips. An electricity composed of anger, grief, pain and a deep, physical desire unfamiliar to her, yet that had caught her by the throat all the same the moment she'd looked into his black eyes.

She'd never been kissed before. She'd never even come close and the thought that her first kiss would be from *him*…

Perhaps that was what she'd unconsciously wanted the moment she'd seen him walking across the sand to her a couple of hours earlier, magnificently naked and so beautiful. A myth made real. Perhaps that was why she'd kept pushing him, telling herself all the while that it was for Aristeidis's sake, when all along it had been because of him. Because the raw, primal power of him had thrilled her, the heat in his black gaze exciting her. The sense that he was dangerous, that he was a threat, was intoxicating and she'd wanted to see how far she could push him before he broke and that threat was made real.

And what a delicious threat he was. His hard mouth on hers, so hot and demanding. She could taste his anger and his desire, and it was thrilling to know it was because of her. Because he wanted her.

She'd spent years viewing him through the lens of her own dim memories and then through that of the media. An enigmatic, brilliant, ambitious man, who'd then retreated from the world stage, whispered about only as rumours and hearsay.

But he was here now and real, so real. His hands were on her hips, holding her fast, his palms burning through the cotton of the T-shirt she wore. His T-shirt. She'd shivered when she'd put it on and smelled his scent, salt and sun and something deliciously musky and masculine.

She shivered again now, surrounded by that same scent, tasting salt as he kissed her, along with a heat that stole her breath. His tongue touched her bottom lip and then pushed inside her mouth, and her head went back, giving him access.

Warmth was beginning to spread through her, a heavy ache gathering between her thighs. She lifted her hands to his chest and spread her fingers out, feeling him, testing his strength beneath the warm cotton of his T-shirt. So hard, like rock.

He deepened the kiss, taking more, like a marauder, and she followed his lead, kissing him back, rewarded when he growled and his hands slid from her hips to the backs of her bare thighs and then up again, moving beneath the hem of her T-shirt. His fingers slipped beneath her underwear, those large, warm palms covering her rear and squeezing, then lifting her up onto her toes as he pulled her hips against his. The hard ridge behind his fly was pressed to the softness between her thighs, making the ache worse and sending a pulse of the most delicious pleasure spiralling through her.

Oh, this felt so good, so much better than the grief and the ache of impending loss she'd been mired in for the past couple of months. This was heaven and she wanted more of it.

She leaned into him, her fingers curling into the soft material of his T-shirt, shifting her hips against his in a blind attempt to get more of that bright, electric pleasure, and he made another deep growling sound in his throat.

He took his hands from her rear, but only to pull the T-shirt off her and discard it onto the floor. Then he ripped her bra off before dealing with his own T-shirt. She didn't stop him—it didn't even occur to her—gasping as he pulled her back for another deep, demanding kiss, her sensitive breasts pressing against his hard, bare chest.

The heat of him was astonishing. His skin felt smooth as oiled silk, with a sprinkle of crisp black hair, and she couldn't stop touching him.

His mouth had made its way down the side of her neck and her head fell back as he found the tender hollow of her throat, his tongue tasting the beat of her quickening pulse. Chills were chasing themselves all over her body, jolts of white-hot electricity making her tremble. His hands slipped down her back and beneath her underwear again, kneading her, pressing her harder against his groin.

In the back of her mind, Elena could hear alarm bells ringing, warning her that this was a terrible idea, that letting grief and anger do her thinking for her was a mistake and life would only get more complicated if she did this with him—especially with him— not less.

But then he made another growling sound and there came a sharp pull and a tearing as he ripped her underwear clean off. His fingers slid through the damp curls between her thighs, fingertips touching her slick flesh, stroking her, sending an intense surge of pleasure through her. And she forgot completely why this was a bad idea, forgot why she was even here.

There was only him and his fingers touching her, gently, delicately, weaving threads of ecstasy through her and making her pant.

'Atticus…' Her voice had become husky and ragged. 'Oh…please…'

He moved again, his hands gripping her hips, and then she was being lifted and carried to the low, comfortable-looking sofa and laid down on it. He ripped off his jeans and his underwear and then that magnificent body was over hers, settling between her thighs. His mouth was at her breasts, his tongue teasing one sensitive nipple before drawing it into the heat of his mouth and sucking hard.

Arrows of pleasure lanced through her and she closed her eyes, trembling as he transferred his attentions to her other breast. She threaded her fingers through his hair, the strands thick and silky against her skin, gasping as he began to work his way down her body, his hot mouth exploring, nipping and licking as he went.

Oh, God, he was going there, wasn't he? He was going to taste her there. She should stop him, she really should, but she didn't want to. She wanted him to keep going, to keep bringing her this blinding pleasure, because she wanted to lose herself in the moment. She didn't want to think.

His strong hands were demanding as they pushed her thighs apart and then she felt his breath against her sensitive skin, his fingers pressing apart her sensitive flesh, baring her for the lick of his tongue.

An intense bolt of ecstasy burst through her as she felt him and she cried out, pushing herself up onto her elbows and looking down, because she wanted to see. She wanted to see what he was doing to her.

His dark head was between her spread thighs, his fingers on her pale skin, and then he glanced up at her, his black eyes full of a dark flame that made her tremble all over again. He looked hungry; he looked like a predator. He looked like a hunter having secured his kill and now he was going to feast. On her.

She couldn't look away as he found the sensitive bud between her legs and teased it, nipping at her and licking. She groaned, her whole body shaking. And when his tongue pushed inside her, tasting her deeply, she screamed as the climax hit her in a white-hot burst.

Elena sagged back onto the sofa, shaking, her mind reeling from the force of it. She couldn't think, every part of her felt deliciously sensitive and raw, as if the pleasure had hollowed her out, leaving nothing behind but a shell.

Dimly she heard him move and the sounds of a packet ripping, and then he was above her, that magnificent rock-hard body settling down on hers. And she found herself looking up into black eyes full of flames, all that dark, predatory hunger focused on her.

She couldn't tear her gaze away as he positioned himself and then he was pushing into her, the unfamiliarity of the feeling making her groan. He was so big, she felt as if there wasn't room for him and her as well, her breath catching in her throat. Sensitive flesh burned as it parted for him and another groan escaped her.

He pushed deeper, his hands sliding beneath her rear, cupping her, lifting her, tilting her hips so he could slide even deeper. 'Elenitsa,' he murmured, his deep voice roughened and full of heat, his gaze on hers. 'Take me.'

And she did, her sex slick and ready for him, and there was no pain, only a feeling of fullness that made her pant. He waited for her to adjust, her hands pressed against his chest, and she was desperate for him to move. 'Please,' she gasped. 'Please... Atticus.'

He must have known exactly what she meant, because he did, deep and slow at first, then getting faster.

More pleasure spread out inside her, along

with a sense of rightness she didn't understand, but didn't question. Because it was
him, and he was inside her, and she felt as if
this was where he was always meant to be.

This myth become a man. Her saviour become her lover.

His beautiful face was taut and she could
see her own pleasure reflected back in his
eyes. He felt this too, she knew it deep in
her soul.

'Atticus.' She touched his face gently, and
then he moved harder, deeper, and the moment was gone, an urgent need replacing it.

His hands encouraged her to move with
him so she did, matching his rhythm as if
born to it, and the spiralling heat began to
gather tighter and tighter.

She lifted her hands to his shoulders, nails
digging into his skin, and then she wrapped
her thighs around his waist, lifting her hips.
He made another of those deep, masculine
growling sounds and lowered his head, taking her mouth, his kiss as hot and as raw as
the movement of his sex within hers.

He moved faster, harder, and she gripped
him tight, pleasure building, a pressure that
was getting too intense to bear. And then just

when she thought she couldn't handle it another second, his hand moved and she felt his fingers slide down between her thighs, to where they were joined, and he slicked his finger over that sensitive bundle of nerves there.

And as if her body were his to command, the pressure fractured and shattered, and she was screaming his name, dimly aware of his own roar of release, as the sky fell down around her and covered her with light.

Atticus lay on the couch, his mind for the first time in years utterly blank, his body full of a delicious lassitude that he hadn't felt in far too long. Years for that too, perhaps? He couldn't remember.

For a moment he didn't move, letting himself drift in blissful silence and enjoying the moment, until slowly awareness began to trickle through him.

Of who the beautifully soft and hot woman lying beneath him was, and why she was here, and that he'd fully lost control of himself, taking her like a beast...

Just like that all the blissful warmth disappeared to be replaced by solid ice.

He'd lost control of himself. He *never* lost control of himself. Never, *ever*.

You remembered a condom at least.

Atticus abruptly shoved himself up and away from her, getting off the couch. His brain was still spinning so he didn't say a word as he went down the hall and into the bathroom to deal with said condom. Then he paused a moment at the basin and splashed some water on his face, trying to get his head clear.

What had he done? What the *hell* had he done?

He'd only wanted to end the conversation, do something about the crackling, fizzing electricity that arced in the air between them. Get rid of the anger inside him that he couldn't seem to leash.

The kiss had been a huge mistake, though at the time it had seemed the only option, and he'd told himself just before his lips met hers that he'd take the kiss, silence her, then push her away. And yet...

The moment he'd felt the softness of her mouth and tasted the sweetness of it, every thought had gone out of his head. There had been only hunger, a raw aching need that had slipped straight through his fingers and out of his control.

It had been so long since he'd felt the soft heat of a woman, so long since he'd touched silky skin and tasted salt and sweetness. She'd been hot, her passion flaring as he'd kissed her, and when he hadn't been able to stop himself from sliding his hands beneath her T-shirt and taking a hold of her satiny giving flesh, pulling her hard against him...

Theos.

She'd shivered, her hands on him, as hungry for him as he was for her, and he'd... lost all sense. His anger had transmuted into sexual desire so quickly and he'd gone up in flames just as she had.

The taste of her was still in his mouth, the slick feel of her sex around his, making him hard again already...

It's Elena. The girl you rescued. The girl your father adopted.

Atticus gripped the sides of the basin, his knuckles white, staring down at it unseeing.

She was the last woman he should have taken, the very last. His father was dying and she was here to bring him home, and he hadn't seen her for sixteen years. And he should have put her on that damn boat the minute she'd got off it, not let her stay, not argue with her, not let the undeniable chemistry between them burn so hot and so bright. And definitely *not* lose his head and take her on the couch in his living room.

She'd been unpractised too, he'd been able to tell, and that was something else he'd conveniently pushed to the back of his mind.

Now you're just going to leave her alone on the couch?

He cursed. He couldn't remember the last time he'd taken a lover—which had obviously been part of the problem—but even when he had, it had only ever been for a night, two at most. He didn't do relationships. A wife and a family would never be in his future. Eleos was and would always be his main concern, which was exactly how he liked it.

Elena was special. She was sacrosanct, and yet…

And yet you took her like a beast.

The porcelain of the basin dug into his fingers. He knew what happened when he lost control of himself, when he allowed his emotions to get the better of him. He made mistakes. How could he have forgotten that?

Taking Elena had been a mistake. A terrible mistake.

And you want to do it again.

No. He couldn't risk it, no matter how much his body might want to. He'd thought his control was perfect, but she'd just blown that little comforting lie to smithereens. Taking her again would only compound the error and further compromise his command over himself. Besides, she was Elena. His Elenitsa. Or at least, she once had been.

Slowly, Atticus forced his fingers to release their grip on the basin. There was no point castigating himself. What was done was done. He'd be a gentleman, though. He wouldn't pretend it never happened or kick her out, but he'd definitely make it clear that it would not be happening again.

Turning from the basin at last, he strode back into the living area. Elena had pulled the T-shirt back on and was now standing once again at the shelves, studying them as if nothing untoward had occurred.

He could almost believe it too if it weren't for the white scraps that littered the floor near the couch, the remains of the underwear he'd torn off her, and the fact that her hair was in a wild golden tangle down her back.

Beautiful...so beautiful...

He gritted his teeth and strode over to where his own clothing lay on the floor, pulling on his jeans and T-shirt as Elena examined the shelves intently.

'Are you okay?' he asked as he pulled up the zip of his fly.

She glanced at him, looking surprised. 'What? Oh, yes, I'm fine.' Except her cheeks were deeply flushed and her mouth was full and red from his kisses, and there was something glittering in her dark eyes. Something that looked like shock.

He came over to her and before she could pull away, he took her face between his hands, tilting her head back slightly so he could study her. 'You are not fine,' he said. 'I'm sorry. That was a mistake.'

She flushed a deeper red. 'If you regret it, I'd really rather not—'

'I didn't say I regretted it,' he interrupted, because, rather to his own surprise, he didn't. 'But it was still a mistake.'

Her expression shuttered and she pulled away, turning to gaze at the shelves again.

'It's fine, Atticus.' The words were casual but it sounded forced. 'It was just sex. No big deal.'

But he suspected it was a big deal all the same.

Another reason why you can't let your control falter, not even for an instant. You are too susceptible to making mistakes.

As if he needed the reminder.

He shoved his hands into his pockets. 'Are you hurt? Do you need—?'

'Like I said, I'm fine.' She gave him another glance and smiled. 'Honestly.' Yet the smile was as forced as her casual tone. There was nothing honest about it.

'You were a virgin, weren't you?'

Another blush stole through her cheeks and her blonde lashes came down, hiding her gaze. 'That's none of your business, but no. I'm not.'

Another lie, he could tell. Which meant she had, indeed, been a virgin.

And you took her brutally fast and hard on the couch.

A thread of shame wound through him.

Theos. He knew what happened when he

allowed his emotions to get the better of him, he *knew*.

Excitement. Inattention. His finger on the trigger. A movement in the trees and a surge of adrenaline. The sound of the gun firing in his ears...

He shoved the memories away, trying to find the obsessive focus that was his normal state of being, the fierce homing-in of his attention that allowed him to detach himself from the past and all the emotions that came with it.

He'd allowed her into his private space, allowed her to distract him from the tasks that normally consumed him here on the island, and that had been his first mistake. He couldn't allow it to continue. The longer he stayed here talking to her, the more distraction would happen, and since he was stuck with her for the night, perhaps it was best for him to absent himself.

'Fine,' he said, allowing her the lie. 'If you need to use the shower, there is one next to the guest bedroom.'

'Thank you.' Still not looking at him, she turned back to her study of the shelves. 'And just so you know, I don't regret it either.'

Another bolt of heat shot through him and he could feel himself getting hard again, wanting more. He could still smell her, taste her, feel the tight, wet heat of her, and the urge to take her stubborn chin and turn her face towards him, to cover her lush mouth with his again, get rid of her T-shirt and take her down onto the floor, was almost too much for him. It took him at least a full minute to wrestle his hunger back into submission.

He didn't say anything, merely turning and heading for the door.

'Don't think I've forgotten what we were discussing,' she said from behind him. 'I still need to talk to you about your father.'

They would not be discussing his father. Not tonight. Not ever.

Atticus ignored her, heading out of the room and into the kitchen, and he forced all thoughts of her and the astonishing pleasure she'd given him from his head, turning his focus onto the dinner he was preparing.

That occupied him fully until he had the fish cooked and a salad prepared, some fresh bread rolls ready to go. By that stage the storm front was nearing, the wind whipping up the palms. He went around the house, closing windows and doors and making sure everything was secure, a process he'd done a thousand times before. The familiarity of the routine soothed him, and by the time dinner was ready and he'd put it on the dining table, he felt more like himself. Cold and focused and intent.

He was just about to call Elena to dinner when his mobile went off. The number was Greek and looked to be from a Kalathes staff member, which was unusual enough that he hit the answer button. 'Kalathes,' he said shortly.

'Mr Kalathes?' a man said. 'I'm afraid I have some bad news.'

Everything inside him tightened. 'What bad news?'

'Your father's health declined quite markedly two days ago, and while the medical staff did everything they could for him, they were ultimately unsuccessful. I'm sorry to say that he died half an hour ago.'

CHAPTER FIVE

ELENA STOOD IN the large, airy salon in the Kalathes villa, the deep blue of the sea through the windows almost aching in its beauty. In fact, the whole island was achingly beautiful, as was the villa that sat on it, all white-washed stone, with many terraces and cool courtyards shaded with vine-covered pergolas.

Kalifos was as far removed from the dusty mountainside town Elena had grown up in as it was possible to get, and she loved it completely. Aristeidis had loved it too.

She and Atticus had just finished scattering some of his ashes in the ocean—as per his request—while the rest had been interred in the Kalathes vault inside the tiny island's church. It had been a beautiful funeral, but there had been no wake. There had been too much media interest and Atticus had been

adamant that he wanted none of them anywhere near the island.

Elena hadn't cared. She'd only wanted to be
sure that Aristeidis had the send-off he'd both
wanted and deserved, since his last wish—
reconciling with his son—hadn't been ful-
filled. Atticus had attended the funeral so
there was that at least.

The lawyer would be here any second to
read the will—Atticus had insisted this be
done as soon as possible—and already Elena
felt exhausted.

She'd been feeling exhausted the whole of
this past week, in fact. Ever since Atticus had
come into the living area of his house in Jamaica, his face white, to tell her that Aristeidis had passed away.

Her adoptive father's health hadn't been
good when she'd left Greece, but he'd insisted
that she go to find Atticus. He'd be fine until
she returned. She shouldn't have listened to
him. She'd been worried about leaving him,
but he'd been so insistent on her finding Atticus that she hadn't been able to refuse when
he'd told her to go.

So she had. She'd gone in search of his son
and while she'd been fighting with Atticus

and then having sex, the only person who'd loved her in the entire world had died, and now she was alone. Again.

She hadn't even had a chance to say good-bye. Again.

At least, Atticus hadn't wasted any time or argued about the need to return to Greece. They'd left Jamaica the next day, and upon arrival on Kalifos, he'd gone straight into organisation mode. He'd been in meetings most of the week with people from his father's company, sorting through what needed to happen with the business, and then more meetings to deal with Aristeidis's finances, and she'd barely seen him. Not that she'd wanted to see him.

She felt as if part of the foundation of her life had fallen away and now everything was unsteady and precarious, and he made everything feel even more so. He was a stranger to her, a fierce, demanding stranger, and now Aristeidis had gone, it was as if she were that eight-year-old girl once more. That girl Atticus had rescued, who'd lost everyone and everything, and who'd been cast on the mercy of someone she didn't know.

Alone in the world yet again.

Her heart tightened and ached. It hadn't helped that she'd had nothing to do since she'd returned, because Atticus had taken over all the organisation. That had galled her, since she'd been handling Kalathes Shipping for a couple of years now due to Aristeidis's illness, but she didn't feel she could protest. Atticus *was* his son after all. She didn't like not having anything to do, however. It left her with too much time to think.

She'd demanded the right to arrange Aristeidis's funeral at least, and Atticus had granted her that. But he hadn't seemed to care that she'd been the one who'd been taking care of Aristeidis for years, who'd become, in essence, his assistant. In fact, Atticus hadn't seemed to care about anything at all. He left the Kalifos villa early in the mornings, taking a helicopter into the Kalathes offices in Athens, and not coming home till late at night, long after she'd gone to bed.

She'd tried to talk to him the few times they'd been in the same room at the same time, but the beautifully carved lines of his face had been hard and set, and his expression forbidding.

A hard, uncompromising man who apparently felt no grief at the death of his father. No grief at not being able to reconcile with him the way Aristeidis had wanted. He didn't seem to let grief touch him at all.

She did, though. She grieved, nursing the thread of anger that ran through her grief. Anger at Atticus. That he hadn't given his father the opportunity to talk, to say goodbye. That he hadn't been able to put a sick, old man ahead of his own issues.

Voices in the hall made her turn from her contemplation of the sea as Atticus and a shorter, older man, silver-haired and in a perfectly tailored suit, entered the salon.

Atticus wore a suit too, black for the funeral and tailored to emphasise his perfect physique. His wide shoulders and broad chest, his narrow waist, lean hips and powerful thighs. Even in a suit, though, there was no hiding the primal vitality of the man who wore it. He radiated it as the sun radiated heat.

Her mouth dried and she tried to ignore the sudden rush of desire that always seemed to occur whenever she was in his vicinity. Just as she tried not to remember that half an hour on the couch in Jamaica, when he'd been inside her, moving deep and hard, giving her the most exquisite pleasure she'd ever experienced.

You can try to forget it, but you'll never succeed.

It was true. Those moments were burned in her brain for ever, hot and bright and overwhelming. She hadn't known what to do when he'd suddenly pushed himself away from her and left the room, her mind still reeling from the effects of that orgasm. She'd never slept with a man before, and she'd felt...devastated in a way she couldn't articulate. As if he'd taken her in those strong, scarred hands of his, broken her into pieces, and then put her back together again in a way that felt wholly new and wholly unfamiliar.

When he'd come back from wherever he'd been and told her it had been a mistake, making it obvious he hadn't felt that same sense of devastation, the only thing that had mattered was that she protect herself. That she give no hint of her own vulnerability.

So she had. She'd told him it was fine, that it was just sex, no big deal.

He hadn't argued. Clearly to him, that was all it had been too.

Yet knowing all of that didn't stop the intense rush of physical desire every time she got close to him. She hated it.

'Elena,' Atticus said in his usual peremptory way, gesturing to the elegant couch upholstered in white linen and scattered with cushions in varying shades of blue. 'You should sit. This won't take long, but you look exhausted.'

The lawyer had already sat himself down in one of the matching armchairs near the couch and was pulling papers out of his briefcase.

Annoyance gripped her, Atticus's high-handedness abrading a temper already rubbed raw with grief and tiredness and a fear she couldn't shake. But snapping at him wouldn't help and she was actually tired. She hadn't been thinking of the will, but, now the time for it to be read was here, part of her didn't want to hear it.

Aristeidis had provided for her, or so he'd said, and she had no idea how and, quite frankly, she wasn't interested. Money seemed like a paltry thing to have instead of Aristeidis himself. She'd rather have had him, rather have had her life here on Kalifos back, than any amount of money.

Atticus sat on the couch beside her, though at the other end, leaving a good amount of distance between them. She tried not to notice that as well.

'Proceed,' he ordered, gesturing at the lawyer.

'Well,' the man said. 'It's all very straightforward. Everything the elder Mr Kalathes had has been left to you, Mr Kalathes.'

'I see,' Atticus said without any discernible expression.

Elena gripped her hands together in her lap. She hoped he'd leave her a few little mementos; that was all she wanted. Some photos perhaps, and maybe one of his handkerchiefs. He'd worn a heavy gold signet ring too, and she wouldn't mind that, though obviously that would probably go to Atticus.

'There's just one tiny complication,' the lawyer went on, 'and it involves Miss Kalathes here.'

Elena frowned. 'What complication?'

The lawyer gave both her and Atticus a rather embarrassed smile. 'Your father stipulated that inheriting his estate, Mr Kalathes,

is contingent on you marrying Miss Kalathes.'

A hot shock went through Elena. She stared
at the lawyer, conscious of Atticus's tense figure down the other end of the couch. 'Excuse
me?' she asked faintly, her brain struggling
to process what he'd said. 'He mentioned that
he'd provided for me, but he'd never said anything about marriage.'

The lawyer spread his hands, looking
apologetic. 'I'm sorry, Miss Kalathes, but he
amended the will just before he died. He was
very concerned that you be taken care of and
because of your…past, he thought Mr Kalathes should be the one to take care of you.'

Elena blinked and opened her mouth, to
say what she wasn't sure, but Atticus got in
first. 'So in order to inherit, I must marry
Elena?' he asked shortly.

'Yes, that's what it says.' The lawyer looked
down at the papers held in his lap, shuffling
through them. 'He specified that the estate
will pass to you once you are married, but
keeping it is contingent on you staying married for at least five years and that children
were to be part of it. Two at the least, either
biological or adopted. Mr Kalathes was very

clear that he wanted Miss Kalathes to have a family of her own.'

Another shock washed through her. Marriage. Children. A family…

Aristeidis had wanted her to have all the things she'd lost.

Her vision swam, her throat aching. He'd thought of her, he really had. He'd said he'd make sure she was provided for…except he wanted Atticus to be her husband.

She didn't dare look at the man at the other end of the couch. He'd gone very still. 'And if we decide not to marry?'

'In that case the estate is to be sold.'

Atticus's features were expressionless. 'Thank you, Mr Georgiou. That will be all.'

The lawyer nodded and Elena was conscious of Atticus rising and talking to him as the man put his papers back in his briefcase, the two of them then walking to the door. Except she wasn't listening, the shock of the will still resonating through her.

There didn't seem to be any end to the shocks she'd been given the past week. First the shock of Atticus's presence and then their one blistering encounter, followed by the bombshell of Aristeidis's death.

She still remembered Atticus's hoarse voice as he'd informed her that Aristeidis had died, seeing the same shock in his eyes that she'd felt and the same grief. Yet his had been momentary. Within five minutes, while she'd shattered, he'd seemed to turn to stone.

He'd made her sit down then too, and had poured her a glass of brandy as she'd wept. But he didn't touch her, not once. And he hadn't touched her since.

She swallowed, another surge of grief hitting her, but she forced it back. She didn't want to cry again in his presence, not when it left her feeling so vulnerable. The marriage idea, while nice that Aristeidis had thought of her, was impossible. She didn't want to marry him, didn't want a family with him, and especially not if the only reason Atticus agreed was because he wanted to inherit his father's estate.

It was true that she longed for a family of her own and always had, but she didn't want anyone forced into marrying her. She wanted what she'd had before her family had died, before Aristeidis had died. She wanted someone to care about her. She wanted someone to love her. And Atticus didn't seem like the kind of man who even knew what love was.

The door shut behind the lawyer and Elena became aware that Atticus had come to stand in front of her, his black handmade leather shoes shiny against the pale wood of the floor.

There was a tight band around her chest, making it difficult to breathe. She didn't want to look up into his face, see that cold, set expression in his eyes. She was used to being strong, yet what she wanted passionately, right in this moment, was someone to hold her. Except she didn't want him to know that.

She couldn't be weak. Back in Jamaica, she'd allowed herself to weep in front of him, but that had been the shock getting to her. She couldn't allow that to happen, not now. Once, long ago, she'd trusted him and he'd abandoned her. And even though she was an adult now and she knew why he had, she still couldn't bring herself to let her guard down with him, not again.

She couldn't rely on him, couldn't trust him as she once had. She only had herself, and the only course left to her was to pull herself together and get on with it. Obviously, she'd have to leave Kalifos. Atticus wouldn't marry her, which meant the entire island and the house with it would go up for sale, and she couldn't afford to buy it. Why Aristeidis had believed his son would fulfil his wishes and marry her, she had no idea. Either way, though, she had nothing.

The thought of losing the only home she'd known for the past sixteen years twisted the knife in her heart, but she ignored the pain. Instead she clasped her hands tightly in her lap and forced herself to look up into Atticus's cold black eyes. 'That's unfortunate,' she said. 'I hope you don't think I had anything to do with it. I had no idea Aristeidis would want to put that in his will.'

Atticus said nothing for a long moment, studying her face. 'No,' he said, his tone impossible to read. 'I'm sure you didn't.'

'Good. Then there's really nothing further to say. I'll collect my things and—'

'No,' he repeated in the same expressionless tone. 'You will not.'

She frowned. 'What are you saying? I can't stay here. The island will have to go up for sale and I—'

'The house will not be going up for sale,'

Atticus interrupted. 'And you will not be going anywhere. This is your home, Elena.'

Her throat closed and she had to force herself to swallow. 'But…but if you want to keep the island, you'll have to…'

'Yes,' he said steadily. 'I'll have to marry you.'

As soon as the lawyer had said the words Atticus had known there was no other option. Even through the shock, and he *had* been shocked—he'd been sure his father would have cut him out of his will the way he'd promised after Dorian had died. Yet apparently not.

Apparently his father had decided to make life even more difficult for both him and Elena. The old man could have just left everything to her and it would have been fine. Atticus wouldn't have cared. He had all the money he'd ever need and Eleos to concern himself with. He didn't need the family shipping company on top of all of that.

But no, Aristeidis had wanted Elena to have a family and expected his son to provide her with one.

Fury at his father had grabbed Atticus by

the throat, and his first, reflexive thought had been to refuse. He'd never wanted a wife and he'd never wanted a family. The island and everything on it would be sold, as would the company, and he'd donate the proceeds to charity as they should, his father be damned.

Yet even as the thought had occurred to him, he knew he couldn't refuse. Elena had spent the past sixteen years here, this was *her* house more than it had ever been his, and she'd already lost her home once. She'd already lost her family, too, and besides, the day he'd rescued her, he'd promised her that he'd look after her.

So while this was a responsibility he hadn't asked for and he was furious about it, he had to accept it. She was his responsibility. She'd always been his responsibility.

He looked down at Elena now, sitting on the couch. She wore full mourning, a black dress with a black veil covering her rich blonde hair. Her attention was on her hands clasped in her lap, her face pale, shadows under her eyes. She looked so small sitting there. Fragile.

This whole week since they'd been back in Greece, she'd been outwardly calm, giving no sign of the grief he'd seen back in his house in Jamaica, where she'd wept on his couch, the glass of brandy he'd given her clutched in her hand. She hadn't been calm then, or the stubborn, challenging, passionate woman he'd taken on that same couch, but a woman fractured by grief.

Something tight had shifted in his chest then, like boulders shifting after a landslide, his own grief stirring. Yet he'd ignored it. He wouldn't cry for his father. He wouldn't grieve. For years he'd tried to reach the old man after Dorian had died, needing his comfort and his reassurance, and he hadn't got it. No, instead all he'd had from Aristeidis was blame.

'You should have died,' Aristeidis had flung at him in those first, terrible days afterwards. *'It should have been you, not him. You.'*

The worst part had been that Atticus had agreed. Yes, it should have been him. But it hadn't. Dorian had been three years older than him. Dorian had known his way around a gun. Dorian had told him all about safety when hunting and to be careful and yet...

All of that had meant nothing, because

Atticus had let the excitement of a hunting trip in the countryside with his adored older brother overwhelm him. He'd seen a movement in the trees and he'd pulled the trigger without thinking. But it hadn't been a deer. It had been Dorian.

He shouldn't hold his father responsible for all the years of blame, for all the years of distance, yet he did. He'd been sixteen when Dorian had died and ill equipped to deal with loss of any kind, let alone to bear the responsibility of killing his own brother. He should have been helped, not accused. Yet his father, still grieving the wife he'd lost nearly fifteen years earlier, hadn't been able to get past it, and he hadn't allowed Atticus to get past it either.

So no, the old man was dead and all he felt was fury. But as he looked at Elena sitting on the couch a ghost of the same protectiveness that had gripped him when he'd first spotted her in the rubble all those years ago gripped him again. Back then she had had a knife in her hand and blood on her face, determined and brave in the face of the threats around her.

She should look like that, not defeated and...broken.

He'd rescued her once and given her a home and a family, and it wouldn't cost him anything to give her another one.

Are you sure about this? Marriage and *fatherhood?*

The thought of fatherhood particularly had unsettled him, which hadn't done his temper any good. Then again, children were part of the stipulation and so why not? He didn't have to be involved in their lives. In fact, it was probably best for all concerned if he wasn't. And as for the getting of said children... Well, he knew that wouldn't be an issue, not with their chemistry.

'You can't be serious,' Elena said, her deep brown eyes still full of shock. 'You can't actually marry me.'

There were definite shadows under her eyes and he could see pain and grief in the tight lines around her lush mouth. She was very pale, the black making her seem even paler, and yet...

Still so beautiful.

'I can,' he said, ignoring the kick of desire inside him that wouldn't seem to leave him alone. There was a reason he'd avoided her since coming back to this place and all the memories associated with it, and, while he had himself under tight control, there wasn't any need to make things any more difficult than they already were. 'And to be clear, it's not the inheritance I want. In fact, once you're my wife, I'll sign ownership of this island and Kalathes Shipping over to you. I have Eleos and don't need anything else filling up my already limited time.'

Those feathery golden lashes fluttered as she blinked yet again. 'So, what? You'll just marry me and give me children and I'll get to stay on Kalifos?'

'Why not? You can manage the company if you so choose, or sell it. I don't care what you do with it. And you'll have the family you always wanted.'

'But…it's marriage, Atticus. We have to stay married for five years. And do you really want children?'

He wasn't sure why she was arguing with him, a bad idea with this knot of temper still sitting in his gut. 'I don't, no. But you want them, I'm assuming?'

'Yes, but—'

'Then what's the problem? I can give you children and you can bring them up on Kalifos. You'll have a family of your own.'

She took a little breath. In her hands was a damp tissue that she'd wadded up and was in the process of tearing apart. 'A family that won't include you.'

'No,' he agreed. 'But I'm not the one who wants a family.'

'And my idea of a family includes the father of my children.'

He lifted a shoulder. 'We can compromise on a few things.'

'You can't *want* to marry me,' she insisted.

'I don't want to marry anyone.' He paused. 'But you should be provided for.'

She glanced away, giving a strange, bitter-sounding laugh. 'So, what? You care about me all of a sudden? After sixteen years? The sex must have been really good.'

Another sharp pulse of anger went through him, though since he'd spent the whole week gripping his emotions by the throat, he certainly wasn't going to release it now.

There was no point giving in to his fury at his father, or at himself for those sixteen years of no contact with her, not even once.

He'd thought she would have forgotten about him, but it was clear she hadn't.

And then you had sex with her, before telling her it was a mistake. She was a virgin, you heard her lie about that, and you let that go, treating her like you'd treat any other of your lovers. She deserved more from you.

He didn't like the feeling that sat inside him, the defensiveness and beneath it the shame. Firstly that he hadn't contacted her while she was growing up and then that he'd let her lie. That he'd taken her on the couch and even now couldn't get the memory of the feel of her skin and the taste of her body out of his head. Her passionate kisses and the way she'd called his name.

You'd like her to be your wife. You'd like to give her children.

He ignored the voice in his head, ignored the desire that still gripped him and the anger that lay burning in his gut. Ignored the way his attention kept focusing on the beat of her pulse in the hollow of her throat and the way the deep V neck of her black dress revealed the soft shadows between her breasts.

'The sex was good,' he said, because she deserved that truth from him at least. 'In fact, the sex was phenomenal. And you're wrong to think I didn't care. I kept tabs on you while you were growing up. I wanted to make sure Aristeidis was looking after you properly.'

She gave him a sudden, piercing look. 'But you never contacted me, not once.'

'No. I…thought it would be better if I didn't.' It was the truth. He had thought that. He'd wanted her to forget him, to forge a relationship with his father instead. 'And I expected you to forget me.'

Emotions flickered over her face, gone so fast he couldn't read them all. But he thought he saw pain and grief and the sparks of something hotter, probably anger. 'Yes, well,' she murmured. 'I didn't forget.' She was still tearing up the tissue in her hands and his gaze kept getting drawn to the neckline of her dress, and he could smell her scent, the tart sweetness of apples. It made him want to take a bite right out of her…

He gritted his teeth. 'Regardless of the past, we need to sort this out now. My offer stands. I rescued you all those years ago, Elena. I wanted to give you a family and a home, and it's not your fault that you've now lost that family and home. You deserve to have another chance at one.'

'So, it's your guilty conscience talking, then.'

Another flicker of anger caught at him, loosening the stranglehold he had on his detachment. 'Does it matter?' He didn't bother hiding the impatience in his voice. 'You need to stay here, where you grew up, and if that means marrying me then I don't see the issue. I can give you everything you ever wanted, Elena. It's only a couple of signatures on a piece of paper. It's no big deal.' He hadn't consciously imitated her saying sex was no big deal, but he heard the echoes of it all the same.

It didn't matter, though. And it *wasn't* a big deal. His focus would always be Eleos, and marriage wasn't going to change that. He wouldn't live here, not in this house full of memories. Memories of the big brother he'd lost and the father who'd turned his back on him. A father who was now gone and good riddance to him.

Don't you regret, even for a moment, not having the chance to speak with Aristeidis before he died?

Something tugged at Atticus, but he ignored it. No, he didn't regret it. Not at all. He'd leave here and go back to Jamaica and his island once he'd married her, and all this was cleared up.

His parents' own marriage had been a loving one, though his mother had died when he was small and he didn't remember her. Sometimes he'd wondered, after Dorian had died, what would have happened if she'd still been alive. Whether his father would have been quite so grief-stricken and determined to take it out on him. Whether he might have had one person who wouldn't have blamed him so completely. But those thoughts weren't productive, since the past was the past and you couldn't change it.

Dorian remembered her though.

Ah, yes. Yet another thing to lay at his door. Dorian's memories of their mother that he had destroyed when he'd mistakenly pulled that trigger. His father had never ceased reminding him about that, either.

Elena was silent. Then, abruptly, she pushed herself up from the couch and moved restlessly over to the windows, looking out over the sea for a moment. Then she turned back to him, her eyes very dark. 'And love? What about that?'

The question caught him off guard. What did love have to do with any of this?

'I don't believe my father mentioned love,' he said coolly. 'He only mentioned marriage. Love has nothing to do with this.' Not that love mattered to him anyway. He'd got rid of that and all the rest of his agonising, useless emotions when he'd turned his back on Kalifos and his father and joined the army.

Love was something that turned on you when you least expected it. Love was unforgiving. Love was vengeful and full of retribution and he wanted nothing whatsoever to do with it.

Elena glanced back out of the window. 'In that case, if it's all the same to you, I'd rather not marry you.'

For a second, all Atticus could do was stare at her. He'd not expected her to refuse him. 'What do you mean you'd rather not marry me?'

'I think it's obvious what I meant. I know your father wanted to provide for me, but I don't want to marry someone who's been forced into it. And I certainly don't want to have a child by that someone.'

His anger pulled against his grip on it. She was *his* responsibility. She had nothing and no one, and he knew what that was like. To have no family at all. But he could provide her with one and he would.

She's right; it is your guilty conscience talking.

Maybe it was, but did that matter? He wasn't going to change his mind. The past week he'd found out from various Kalathes staff members that Elena had taken over managing various aspects of Kalathes Shipping as his father's health had declined. It had been with his blessing and she'd been an astute and capable manager. Whether she enjoyed the work, he wasn't sure, but, regardless, all the more reason it should be in her name.

'It was not a request,' he said. 'If you want Kalifos, if you want the company, there's only one way for that to happen and that's by marrying me.'

'You're assuming I want those things.'

Atticus opened his mouth to send back a sharp reply, but then bit down on it. Her temper sparked too easily off his and he was allowing it. He liked arguing with her, but that wasn't helping.

Anger isn't the only thing you spark, remember?

A thick, hot feeling shifted inside him. That was true. Perhaps there was…another way to get her agreement. A way that would end up being far more pleasurable for both of them than bickering.

'I know what you want, Elenitsa,' he murmured, letting his voice drop.

She gave him a glance. 'Oh, yes? What?'

He held her melted-chocolate gaze with his. 'Me.'

CHAPTER SIX

THE WORD SPOKEN in his deep, dark voice sent a lightning strike of heat straight down Elena's spine. His gaze was electric, full of sparks and black flames, as if he'd suddenly thrown open a door and all the light and heat inside were spilling out.

There had been nothing but that tight band of grief locked around her chest and yet, looking at him now, she forgot all about it.

He dominated the room, filled it with the intense, primal energy she'd felt back on his island. The black suit he wore fitted him so perfectly, yet he might as well have been naked. It couldn't contain him or his presence.

He's right. You do want him.

She swallowed, her mouth gone dry. 'No,' she said, lying through her teeth. 'No, I don't.'

He raised one dark brow. 'I see. So you don't want me just like you weren't a virgin?'

Did you really think he wouldn't know what a liar you are?

She could feel the flush creep up her neck and into her cheeks. She'd suspected he knew that she'd lied to him about her virginity, but since he hadn't called her on it, she'd told herself that maybe her suspicions were wrong.

Sadly they were not wrong.

She wanted to deny it, tell him she wasn't lying, but, with that black gaze holding hers, she knew that would only be making the hole she was digging for herself even deeper.

'Fine,' she snapped. 'I was a virgin. But I'm not lying about wanting you. We had sex and it was great, but I don't necessarily need to revisit it.'

He said nothing for a long moment, still studying her. Then he took a few casual steps in her direction and every muscle in her body tightened in response, her heartbeat thumping hard in her head.

'Don't you?' His voice was just as casual as the slow way he approached her. 'Are you sure you couldn't be tempted to revisit it?'

He wasn't being threatening. His hands

were in the pockets of his trousers, his posture relaxed, and yet… She could feel the intense sexual energy he was radiating and it made her go hot with reaction. There was a pulse of heat between her thighs, a dragging ache. She couldn't seem to get a breath.

'N-no,' she said, hating the way she stuttered and how breathy her voice sounded. 'I mean… I'm… I'm sure.'

His black gaze settled on hers, full of intent and a dark hunger that she knew he was letting her see on purpose. It made the ache inside her get worse. 'There's no purpose in lying, Elena,' he murmured. 'Because I can see what I do to you. I *know* what I do to you. I was there, remember? I heard the way you called my name as you climaxed. Twice, wasn't it?'

She knew she should look away, turn and walk from the room, get out of his vicinity somehow, but she couldn't seem to move. She was caught in his gaze like a deer in the headlights of a car, utterly frozen. And not just caught by her own need, but by the need she saw in his face too. Need for her.

'I'm not the only one,' she said huskily. 'I do the same to you.'

'That's true.' He moved again, coming even closer, until he was mere inches away. And she could smell him once again, salt and sun and masculine spice, so delicious. He wore a deep blue silk tie with his black shirt, the colour highlighting the tanned olive skin of his strong neck, and suddenly all she could think about was undoing that tie and taking it off, pulling at the top buttons of his shirt and uncovering his skin. Tasting the hollow of his throat the way he'd tasted hers.

'In which case...' He reached out, putting one long finger beneath her chin, tipping her head back, and she didn't pull away, trapped by the force of her hunger and by the sheer charisma of his presence. 'Why not give us what we both want? Marrying me wouldn't be all bad, Elenitsa. You'd get the island, the company, and, while I have no plans to live here, I could certainly spend some time consummating our marriage.'

Her heartbeat got louder and louder. She couldn't tear her gaze from his. The heat from his finger beneath her chin felt as if it were burning into her, the warmth of his body and the scent of him making every part of her go weak with hunger.

Would it really be so bad? No, it's not love, but then you don't love him. You don't need him to stay here on Kalifos, either. And you'd be fulfilling Aristeidis's last wish, which is to make sure you're provided for.

It was true, she would. Aristeidis had wanted to give her a family and it seemed petty of her to deny him that just because Atticus unsettled her and because she was holding out for love. Especially after Aristeidis been denied a reconciliation with his son. Also, she hadn't been there when he'd died; she hadn't even been able to say goodbye. Surely she couldn't refuse to fulfil at least *one* of his dying wishes. Besides, they didn't even need to be together for ever, since the will stipulated they had to stay married for only five years. She could find the love she wanted with someone else after that.

'I… I don't know.' Her voice had become so husky, giving her away. 'Do you even want to consummate our marriage?'

His hard mouth curved and abruptly she could see the desire that burned hot and strong in his gaze. 'I wouldn't have offered if I didn't want to. For the record, there isn't one person on this planet who can force me into doing what I don't want to do.'

Something about that half-smile made her breath catch. He'd been nothing but focused and very intense since the day she'd met him, and she wouldn't have thought he'd even known what a smile was, but it seemed that he did. And it was mesmerising. She couldn't stop looking at it.

'Yes,' she heard herself say. 'I think I already know that about you.'

His thumb moved, tracing her bottom lip, pushing gently against the softness, making her heart beat even faster. 'Good. Then you'll know that there isn't anything I'd like better than to give you a suitable wedding night.'

She swallowed, her bottom lip feeling acutely sensitised. 'Atticus…'

He gripped her chin and bent his head, his mouth brushing over hers, and her brain blanked, the electricity of the kiss making even the air around her crackle and spark.

His fingers tightened and he kissed her again, as if he couldn't help himself, his mouth lingering, coaxing her to open. And she did, unable to stop herself, letting him deepen the kiss.

He tasted so good and she was tired of grief, tired of looking into the future and seeing nothing but loneliness, nothing but having no one and nowhere to call home, no connections with anyone or anything. She wanted this, the heat of his mouth and the glory of his touch. The need she saw in his eyes. And she could stay on Kalifos, which was home to her, and where she had a purpose.

So why not marry him? Why not have this? She could have him. He would be her husband for a few years and he'd give her children. She'd have a family in the end. It was what she'd always wanted and what Aristeidis had wanted for her too, so why not?

Elena opened her mouth, let the kiss get hotter. Let him tip her head back further, explore her deeper. She kissed him back, the rich taste of him filling her head, dark chocolate and mint. It felt like balm to her wounded soul, and she found her hands lifting, reaching for him.

Abruptly, though, he released her, lifting his head and looking down into her eyes. 'Is that a yes?' His voice was rough, and she could hear the edge of demand in it.

She swallowed, her fingers itching to touch

him, her whole body aching with desire. Part of her didn't want to give in so easily, though, still half angry with him over so many years of silence, a silence that she hadn't thought she'd care about and yet apparently still did. Angry, too, that he had the power to unsettle her, to make her feel vulnerable when she didn't want to be.

'I don't know,' she said huskily. 'Is that a proposal?'

His black eyes glittered and suddenly his hands dropped to her hips and she was being pushed firmly but gently up against the wall. The breath went out of her as he looked down into her eyes. 'If it's a proposal you want, then here it is. Marry me, Elenitsa.'

It wasn't a request, it was an order; she could hear the edge of command in his voice. The stubborn part of her wanted to refuse, the lost girl who'd been abandoned by him and still felt that abandonment even years later. But she wasn't that girl any more. She wasn't a child. Marrying him wouldn't mean anything, not if she didn't want it to, and if it would get her what she wanted then why not?

He'd been the soldier who saved her, the prince, a fairy tale, a cipher. He'd never been a person to her, only a stranger. She didn't know him now either, and so why she was letting him get to her so intensely, she had no idea.

Still, she didn't see why all the power should be with him. She liked pushing him, liked testing herself against him. Found the sensual threat he presented and the sparks they created between them intensely exciting.

He unsettled her and she didn't see why she shouldn't return the favour. If she could…

She looked up at him from beneath her lashes, wanting him to know that he wasn't going to get it all his own way. 'Convince me,' she said, then reached up and began to undo his tie.

Atticus stared down into Elena's darkening brown eyes. They were liquid with desire and her cheeks were flushed. The pulse at the base of her throat was fast and getting faster, and the heat of her body against his was rapidly making it impossible to think.

He wasn't sure why she was so determinedly holding out against him, because he knew she wanted him and badly. He hadn't been wrong about that. So was it only because she liked arguing with him, or was it really about the past still? Or was there more going on here than he thought, something else?

Her fingers tugged at his tie, pulling the silk out of its knot, and he let her. He was still in command of himself and he'd stay in command, no matter how hot her mouth tasted or how soft her body felt.

She dropped the tie onto the floor then began undoing the top buttons of his shirt, pulling open the cotton and baring his throat.

'Seems like you're already convinced,' he murmured.

'But I haven't said yes yet.' She put her hands on his chest and rose up onto her toes, putting her mouth at the base of his throat.

All his muscles tightened, desire pulsing like a giant heartbeat inside him. Her little tongue touched his skin, tasting him, and her lips were so soft. The pressure of her hands on his chest felt maddening. He wanted to feel her bare skin on his, because he could still remember how silky it had been and how hot. How sweet it had tasted, too.

And why not? If she was going to be his wife, there wasn't any reason why they couldn't fully indulge in the sexual attraction that burned between them. If they had to stay married for five years and there was a stipulation for children, then they were even obligated to indulge themselves. He certainly wasn't going to remain celibate all that time, not when he very much wanted her.

She's already made you lose control once. She'll do it again if you're not careful.

No, she wouldn't. True, he'd been taken off guard a week ago when she'd first turned up and he hadn't managed himself well. But he was prepared for his attraction to her now, he could control it. In fact, it would be easy. No doubt after five years it would burn itself out. In fact, he'd be surprised if it lasted beyond a year. Sexual infatuations always did, not that he'd ever been sexually infatuated with anyone.

Still, maybe this would be a good test for himself, and he did like testing himself. He did it constantly on the island, testing himself physically against the elements. He'd done so in the army too, after Dorian had died, applying to join the elite sniper unit. Handling a gun again had filled him with dread and yet he'd forced himself to become comfortable with it. He'd wanted to master his fear, wanted to master himself, so he'd never again be in a situation where he wasn't in control. Where he wasn't in complete command of the situation and of himself.

Becoming a sniper had been hard, both physically and emotionally, but he'd pushed himself to become the best they'd had. The coldest, the deadliest. No life was taken except when he willed it and he made no mistakes. Mistakes were unforgivable.

He'd made a mistake back in Jamaica in allowing his physical hunger to overcome him, but he wouldn't make the same mistake now. She could do whatever she wanted to him. He wouldn't break.

If he could pick up a gun again after Dorian had died, he could do anything at all.

She undid another button and then another, baring his skin to her kisses. He could hear her breathing getting faster and faster, could feel his own hunger tightening. He was getting hard, the beast in him urging him to push her against the wall, haul her dress up and get inside her as quickly as he could.

He ignored the feeling, putting his hands to the wall on either side of her head and pressing against it.

She pulled open the buttons of his shirt completely, baring his chest, her hands stroking him, following the lines of his pecs and down to his abs, caressing him as if he were a work of art and she were breathless before him.

Her fingertips were cool and he could smell her scent, sweet musk and apples, and a possessive growl formed in his throat. Then her fingers stroked lower, to the button of his trousers, and the growl rumbled in his chest, a low, rough sound.

It was getting harder not to touch her, not to rip away her veil and loose her hair. Not to force her head back and kiss her, taste her sweetness and heat. But no, he could bear this. There was no rush. He wasn't going to take her like an animal the way he had last time. In fact, he might not take her at all. He wanted to, badly, but his body didn't get to decide his actions. Only his mind did.

Her fingers were undoing his trousers now, finding the tab of his zip and taking hold of it.

'What are you doing, Elenitsa?' he asked in a voice that was much rougher than it should have been. 'I thought I was supposed to be the one convincing you?'

'I changed my mind.' Slowly she drew down his zip, glancing up at him from beneath her thick golden lashes. 'I think I need to convince myself.'

He gritted his teeth against the sudden rush of hunger. 'Convince yourself of what? If it's that I'll give you pleasure, then you found that out pretty thoroughly last week.'

She held his gaze as she slid her hand into his trousers, caressing the hard length of him through the cotton of his underwear. Electricity crackled through him at her light touch, making his breath catch. It was maddening.

He had his hand over hers, pressing her palm harder against him before he'd even thought straight, and when he saw an answering flare of heat in her eyes, he suddenly realised exactly what she was doing.

'What do you want?' he demanded roughly. 'To push me? Is that what you're doing?'

'No.' She didn't pull her hand away. Instead she squeezed him gently, making him give another helpless growl, her dark eyes full of determination and heat. 'I only wanted to give you a taste of your own medicine.'

Ah, so that was it. She didn't like how hungry she was for him and so was hoping to return the favour. Little witch.

It's working.

Well, he was hungry for her, yes, but not beyond all sense. He was in control of this and his own body. He wasn't going to lose it. He could pull away from her whenever he wanted, and, in fact, maybe he should do it now. Just to prove his point.

Except he didn't.

'If you really want to give me a taste of my own medicine,' he heard himself say, 'then perhaps get down on your knees.'

It was a challenge, he couldn't say it wasn't. Since she was challenging him with her maddening touch and her soft mouth, then he would do the same to her. He told himself that she wouldn't do it, that she'd baulk. She was inexperienced, after all, and perhaps this would be a step too far for her.

But deep down, he knew she wouldn't baulk. Not Elena. Elena, who'd held five men at bay with a knife, at eight years old. Who'd survived on her own in the ruins of her village for a week before he'd found her, somehow finding food and water, and managing to avoid looters and all kinds of other people who'd do her harm.

Something hot lit in her gaze and slowly she obeyed, going down onto her knees in front of him.

He couldn't take his eyes off her as electricity crackled through him, desire tightening its grip. She looked perfect kneeling on the floor, gazing up at him, her eyes dark, her mouth full and lush and red. Her hands went to his underwear, pulling it down and taking him out without hesitation. Then her cool fingers were on him, stroking him.

Atticus reached for her veil without thinking, pulling it off so he could push his fingers into the silky wealth of her hair. She shuddered as he did so, but didn't hesitate as she leaned forward to take him in her mouth.

He couldn't stop the groan that escaped, or the fierce rush of pleasure that flooded through him as the heat of her mouth enveloped him.

She will *make you lose control. You can't stop her.*

No, it was worse than that. He didn't want to stop her. He wanted her to keep going. He wanted the heat of her mouth and the pressure, the feel of her teeth against his aching shaft and the exploration of her tongue.

'Elena,' he growled as she began to explore, licking him, teasing him.

She only looked up, her eyes dark, the flush in her cheeks creeping down her neck and down beneath the neckline of her dress. It was the most erotic sight, watching her swallow him as she knelt in front of him, her own hunger for him blazing in her eyes.

He gripped her hair tighter, murmuring to her, and she set up a rhythm in response with a confidence that left him breathless as the pleasure began to tighten inside him.

Her mouth was hot and felt so good, and he couldn't think why he'd wanted to hold out against her. He couldn't seem to think at all. Nothing was working right, only the heat of her mouth and the pleasure she was giving him mattered. Only the silky feel of her hair between his fingers and the thrust of his hips.

She made a soft throaty sound, as if she was enjoying this as much as he was, and then the pressure increased as she took him deeper. Then he was thinking about nothing but the ecstasy she was giving him, indescribable, unstoppable, and dimly he was aware that somehow, at some point, the control he was so proud of had escaped his grip. But by then he didn't care.

He roared her name as abruptly the pleasure contracted like a fist around him and crushed him into dust.

CHAPTER SEVEN

ELENA ADJUSTED THE drape of the wedding gown and stared at herself in the bedroom's full-length mirror. She couldn't speak, a complicated knot of emotion sitting heavy in her chest and closing around her throat.

She would be marrying Atticus tomorrow, a week to the day since she'd knelt for him in the salon and taken him in her mouth. A week since she'd made him lose control. And a week since he'd hauled her to her feet, pushed her up against the wall, pulled her dress up and had taken her again within minutes.

They hadn't spoken afterwards yet that night there had come a knock on her door, and when she'd opened it, she'd found him standing on the other side. He hadn't said a word, but his gaze had been fierce and hot, making it obvious what he'd wanted.

She'd had a half-second where she'd considered refusing him and then that half-second had passed and she'd thrown the door open, stepping aside to let him enter. Because she'd wanted what he'd wanted and every bit as badly.

He'd come to her door every night since and every night she hadn't refused him. They didn't talk. There wasn't any need to. The only language they needed was that of passion and pleasure, hunger and desire.

During the day, they barely saw each other. He was busy dealing with Eleos, so she took over handling the intricacies of Kalathes Shipping, as well as planning the wedding, which they both wanted to occur as quickly as possible.

She'd asked him if he had any preferences on the type of wedding he wanted and he'd told her that he didn't care as he had no one he wanted to invite, though he did insist on no media coverage.

She was fine with that. She had no one to invite either, though she'd decided she wanted more than the register office wedding that Atticus had suggested. She'd lost many important things in her life, but a lovely wedding gown, a beautiful church, wedding rings and a ceremony weren't going to number among those things. They weren't marrying for love, but for a will, it was true, but she wanted the trappings of a true wedding all the same. She'd even insisted on a honeymoon.

Atticus hadn't argued. The only thing he seemed to want was her, at least physically. He'd been insatiable, glutting himself every night on her, keeping her up until the small hours of the morning. She hadn't minded, not when she'd been just as obsessed as he was. The things he'd taught her, the things they did together...

They made her feel hot to think about, they made her feel hungry. *He* made her feel hungry. As if the more she had of him, the more she wanted. She hadn't realised sex could be like that, and she wasn't sure she liked it. It made her feel vulnerable, as if she needed him, and she didn't like the idea of needing him. Then again, she didn't want to stop and there was no reason to anyway. He was going to be her husband and since children had been part of Aristeidis's will, they had to be conceived somehow.

The emotion that constricted her throat

tightened further as she looked in the mirror. She couldn't tell if what she felt was grief, regret, happiness or anger. Maybe it was a combination of all of them. Grief that her long-ago family weren't around to see her get married. That her father wouldn't be able to give her away, neither would Aristeidis. Regret that Aristeidis was gone, that he wouldn't see her marry his son.

Happiness that here she was in the most beautiful wedding gown she'd ever seen, and she felt good in it, and she would have a veil and flowers, and it would be the wedding she'd always dreamed of.

Anger that she was wasting all of this on a man she didn't love and who didn't love her.

Then again, without that man, she wouldn't even be having a wedding, let alone a wedding dress like this, with acres of white silk and frothy tulle, rising up into a strapless bodice with a deep V neckline that showcased her pale shoulders and breasts. There were tiny crystals embroidered onto the skirts that glittered and sparkled whenever she moved, as if stars had fallen all over her and had become caught in the fabric.

Do you really deserve this? After you let a

complete stranger take you away to a pampered life in Greece, while your family lay dead beneath the rubble?

The old doubts whispered unexpectedly in her head, chilling her, but she forced them aside. What was she supposed to have done? She'd been eight and all alone. She'd had to leave them behind; she'd had to.

Anyway, what was done was done, and she couldn't think about it now.

Elena stared at her figure in the mirror, blinking fiercely against the prickle of silly emotional tears.

Atticus would like it, she was sure, but there wouldn't be any other, deeper emotion attached to it for him. He wasn't marrying her because he loved her and wanted her to be his wife. He was marrying her to provide for her, because he felt obligated towards her due to his father's will, and that wasn't the same.

You weren't supposed to care whether he loved you or not.

And she didn't. Not at all. It was only that a wedding was supposed to be a celebration of love and theirs wouldn't be a celebration of anything.

So what's the point of all this? The dress

and the church? The rings and flowers? You might just as well have got married in a register office.

Elena tore her gaze from the mirror and adjusted the bodice needlessly. There *was* a point to this. The gown and the little church on Kalifos where they were going to be married, the rings…all of those things were for her, because she wanted them. She'd lost everything that mattered to her once and then she'd lost it again after Aristeidis had died. She wasn't going to let it happen again. She wanted a home and a family and everything that went with it, and that included a proper wedding. That mattered to her.

You won't have a proper husband though.

Elena forced the thought away as a knock sounded on the bedroom door.

Gathering her skirts, she went over to it, opening it a crack, not wanting anyone to get a glimpse of her gown.

It was Atticus.

The sight of him sent first a shock, then a shiver of pure heat straight through her. She wasn't expecting him, not now, not so early in the evening. He wasn't supposed to come until well after dinner had been finished and the sky was dark.

Yet here he was and her pulse was already beginning to pick up, her mouth getting dry. He wore one of the handmade suits that looked so stunning on him, this one in a deep, dark blue wool, bordering on black. The colour was fantastic against his tanned skin, as was the white of his shirt. He wasn't wearing a tie and the top buttons of his shirt were undone and immediately all she wanted was to press her mouth to his throat.

His eyes glittered—clearly he knew exactly what she was thinking.

'You're early,' she said, feeling herself blush, which was ridiculous considering all the things they'd done together over the past week.

'I need to talk to you.' His gaze dropped to her bare shoulders. 'Though, if you're naked, I can think of something else I'd much rather do first.'

Much to her annoyance, she could feel her blush deepen. 'I'm not naked, but I need a minute to change.'

'I can help with that.'

A strangely vulnerable feeling stole

through her. She didn't want him to see her in her gown, not yet, which was silly considering he wouldn't care. But still, she'd wanted a proper wedding and the groom not seeing the bride in her gown before the wedding was a tradition.

'No,' she said, not wanting to explain it to him. Her emotions and reasons were too complicated and she didn't want to go into it.

He frowned. 'Why not?'

'Because you'll only...distract me. Give me five minutes.' And she closed the door in his face before he could get another word in.

She managed to get the zip down and then carefully stepped out of the gown, making sure to put it back in its protective garment bag and hang it back in her wardrobe. She half expected Atticus to ignore her and come in anyway, but he didn't.

Finally, pulling on some soft yoga pants and a white cotton T-shirt, she went back over to the door and opened it wide, standing aside to let him enter. '*Now* you can come in.'

He went past her into the room, his gaze narrowing as he looked around, as if she'd been hiding something from him and he wanted to know what it was.

'I don't have a lover stashed under the bed or in the wardrobe,' she said tartly, still feeling vulnerable and not liking it one bit. 'If that's what you're worried about.'

His black gaze settled on her and once again she felt the build-up of electricity, the intense static charge of their attraction in the air around them. Surely it shouldn't still be so intense by now? They'd slept together every night for the past week; she couldn't still be so hungry for him, could she?

'No.' His voice had deepened with a very male kind of satisfaction. 'That's the very last thing I'd be worrying about.'

Excitement and annoyance knotted inside her. Excitement at his presence and annoyance at his arrogance, as if he was completely and utterly confident that the last thing she'd have was another lover somewhere.

He was right, though, she didn't. In fact even the thought of being with another man left her cold, which he didn't need to know since he was already arrogant enough as it was.

'I might have another lover,' she said, unable to help herself. 'You don't know.'

'I do know and if you want me to prove

it, I'd be happy to.' He was already taking a step towards her, flames in his eyes, but she held up her hand, discomfited by the sudden burst of desire she felt.

She had to give him some boundaries somewhere, otherwise she'd let him have everything he wanted, and she wasn't starting off their marriage like that. In fact, come to think of it, she really should talk to him at some point about what their marriage *would* look like, especially since they were supposed to stay married for five years.

She didn't want him thinking she'd give in every time he wanted her. She wasn't *that* available.

Elena was just about to open her mouth to tell him not now, when he stopped his advance towards her. 'As much as I'd like to put your bed to good use, that can wait. I have something to give you.' He put his hand into the pocket of his trousers and brought something out of it. A small black velvet box.

She stared, the thick weight of emotion in her chest getting even thicker, even heavier, because that was a ring box. Why would he be giving her a ring box? She'd got one of the best ring designers she could find to design their wedding rings and he knew that. So this couldn't be a wedding ring.

'What is it?' she asked after a couple of moments.

Atticus merely continued to hold it out to her. 'Open it.'

Slowly, she took the box from his hand and lifted the lid. A man's heavy golden signet ring gleamed against the black velvet.

Aristeidis's ring.

Elena lost her voice completely, staring at the ring then meeting his gaze.

The expression in his dark eyes was very direct. 'Aristeidis wanted you to marry me so that you could be taken care of, and it seemed appropriate, since he isn't here, that you have his ring as an engagement ring. Unless you'd prefer something more feminine?'

Another rush of emotion took her, so intense she couldn't have spoken even if she'd wanted to. Helpless, pathetic tears filled her eyes, her vision swimming, and she had to blink them back fiercely, because she didn't want to cry in front of him, not again.

'I'll have something else made if you don't like it,' Atticus went on, frowning as if he'd spotted her tears. 'You shouldn't have to buy your own engagement ring at least.'

It was clear he thought she didn't like it, when in fact the opposite was true. It was Aristeidis's ring, the one she'd hoped to have passed on to her when his will had been read, but she'd thought Atticus might want it. It was a man's ring after all.

'How did you know?' Her voice was way too hoarse and the question revealed more than she wanted it to, but she couldn't help it. 'How did you know I wanted this?'

Atticus's dark gaze flickered, the frown disappearing. He studied her for a long moment. 'He meant a lot to you, I know that. He brought you up, he was a father to you. And you meant a lot to him. I think he would have wanted you to have his ring and I can't think of a more appropriate occasion than to have it as an engagement ring.'

She was shocked that Atticus had thought about it. That he'd thought of her and Aristeidis, of what he'd meant to her and she to him, and had come up with a gesture so lovely and so meaningful that her heart ached with a bittersweet grief.

'He wanted to give me away at my wedding,' she said huskily, staring at the ring. 'And I wanted him to.'

Atticus was silent a moment, then he came towards her and took the box from her shaking hand, extracting the ring. He put the box back in his pocket and then took her hand.

'It'll be too big,' she said, suddenly feeling horribly fragile. 'It'll be too big and I—'

Without a word, Atticus slid the ring onto her finger. It fitted perfectly.

'I had it resized for you,' he said.

Despite her best efforts, a tear slid slowly down over her cheek as she stared at the ring, but she resisted the urge to brush it away. Perhaps if she ignored it, Atticus wouldn't notice. 'You don't want it for yourself?' she asked, keeping her gaze on the soft glow of gold around her finger.

'No. He was a better father to you than he ever was to me.' After a moment, he went over to her dresser, where there was a tissue box. Taking a couple of tissues out, he came back then took her chin in one hand and tilted her head back so she was looking at up him.

She didn't want him to see her tears, to see her vulnerability, but his hold was gentle and she didn't resist as he began to carefully wipe her tears away.

Elena trembled. She felt raw all of a sudden, yet his touch was very kind, with none of his usual sexual demand in it, and, strangely, she found herself relaxing in his hold. She still couldn't meet his gaze, though. Her instinct was to say something sharp or pull away to protect herself, but part of her liked the gentle way he was touching her far too much.

Aristeidis had cared about her, but he'd never been physically affectionate. He'd never given her hugs. And he'd never known what to do when she cried, so she'd soon learned that if she wanted something from him, it was best not to cry. It was best not to look as if she needed anything at all. It wasn't that he was negligent or cruel. He just wasn't physically affectionate and outward displays of emotion made him uncomfortable.

So Atticus taking care of her like this, giving her a gift that meant something to her and then wiping her tears away… It set up a painful ache deep in her heart, the tug of a need she hadn't realised she still felt, a weakness she couldn't allow herself.

Yet still she stood there, letting him touch her.

'You know that, not only will the island be yours,' he murmured, giving her face a critical examination as he wiped away the last of her tears, 'but everything in it will also be yours, too.'

She swallowed, half sad when he finally released her chin, half relieved. 'There must be something that *you* want here, though,' she said.

He put the tissue in a waste basket near her dresser. 'No. I don't want any of it.'

'Why not?' It wasn't the best thing to be discussing now, but she still felt overly emotional and she didn't want to answer any questions he might ask her. Much better to turn the conversation back on him. 'I would have thought you might—'

'I said no.' The concern he'd shown her just before was gone, only annoyance snapping in his black eyes.

'It's because of Dorian, isn't it?' She wasn't going to regret the loss of that concern. His anger she could deal with far better than his tenderness. 'And because of what happened afterwards?'

Instantly Atticus's expression went hard

then it blanked completely. 'I don't want to discuss this now.'

She shouldn't push. It would only ruin the moment and make things difficult between them, which, considering they were getting married in the morning, wasn't a great start. And anyway, she was suddenly tired of arguing with him, tired of things being difficult between them.

'Okay,' she said simply, dropping the subject.

Surprise flickered over his features. Clearly he'd expected an argument, and it gave her a brief thrill of satisfaction that she could upset his expectations and take him off guard in a way that wasn't sexual.

In fact, she wanted to do it again.

'Wait there,' she said, holding up a finger. Then she went over to her dresser and pulled open a drawer. She'd been saving the small wedding gift she'd had made for him until tomorrow, but he'd given her Aristeidis's ring and she wanted to give him something in return now.

Taking out the small box in the drawer, she turned and came over to him. His gaze narrowed as she approached, and a wave of

unfamiliar shyness overcame her. What if he
didn't like it? Or what if it wasn't meaningful to him? She didn't know him, that was the
issue. Oh, she knew about his boyhood here
on Kalifos, because Aristeidis had told her all
about it, stories of him and Dorian and the
things they used to get up to, the scrapes they
got into. Atticus loved the outdoors, and was
always the more boisterous of the two, Aristeidis used to say. The naughtiest, the more
high-spirited, and the one who took the most
risks. A typical youngest child, whom, by his
own admission, Aristeidis had been harder
on than Dorian.

'I have something for you, too,' she said
and held out the box.

He stared at it as if he'd never seen a box
before in his entire life. 'Something for me?'
The disbelief in his voice was palpable.

She smiled, pleased that she'd managed to
shock him, because there was no doubting
the shock on his face. 'It's a wedding gift. I
was going to give it to you tomorrow, but you
may as well have it now.'

'A wedding gift,' he repeated, as if the
words were foreign to him. 'But…this isn't a
real wedding, you know that, Elena.'

'I know. But that doesn't mean we can't have the trappings of one. And you're still going to be my legal husband, whether it's real or not, and so I wanted to get you a gift.'

He stared at her for a long moment, then reached out and took the box from her hand. Her heartbeat sped up, nervousness kicking in. She hadn't realised how much she wanted him to like this, but she did. His opinion mattered.

Slowly he took the box in his large hands, the scars standing out whitely against his olive skin, and he opened it, staring down at the small item sitting in the black velvet.

It was a pin crafted out of platinum, of a small child with their arms lifting up as if for someone to carry them. The Eleos symbol.

He stared at it, his face utterly unreadable, and nerves crowded in her throat. 'It's just a little thing,' she said quickly, desperate to fill up the silence. 'It's probably silly. You've probably got hundreds of them and you don't—'

'I don't,' he interrupted, still staring down at the pin. 'I don't have a single one.' Then he looked up at her, an emotion she didn't understand burning in his black eyes. 'Where did you get this?'

'I had it made. I wanted to give you a gift that meant something to you, but I don't know you well enough and I…' She trailed off, because he was still staring at her, a fierce storm in his eyes.

'Do you know what this is?' he asked.

Her heart was beating faster and she didn't know what to say, because she wasn't sure whether he liked it or not, or whether she'd somehow offended him. 'Yes, it's the symbol of your charity.'

'It's not just the symbol of my charity.' A bright, intense flame glowed in his eyes. 'It's also you, Elena.'

Perhaps he shouldn't have said it. Perhaps he shouldn't have revealed something so personal. But it was too late now. He'd told her, he hadn't been able to help it. She'd given him this pin, a symbol of his charity, a symbol of hope. Because she'd been his hope.

That night in the rubble of that town, surrounded by death and hopelessness, he'd wondered what the point of it all was. He'd been involved in the business of violence for years and he was starting to lose himself. He was starting to think that maybe there was no difference between himself and those he was protecting people from. After all, he was a killer just as they were. What made him different? What made him a good person? He'd killed his brother, been repudiated by his father... Was there anything good in him at all?

A black despair had been creeping up on him, and that was when he'd seen her, a small figure fighting back against impossible odds. Indomitable. Unbroken. Her braids had been lit by the setting sun, gleaming gold, and the blood on her face had made her look fierce. She'd been so small and yet there she was, fighting back against the dark.

He'd felt something leap inside him in that moment and he'd known immediately that he had to save her and that if he had to die to do so, then die he would. He'd lifted his weapon and fired the warning shots and her attackers had scattered, and he'd been expecting her to run from him too.

Yet she hadn't. She'd lifted her arms to him as if she'd been waiting for him, as if she wasn't afraid of him. As if she knew completely that he would pick her up and take care of her.

As if she could see that there was some part of him that was still good.

She'd had no idea what she'd meant to him that evening. No idea how she'd turned his life around. After he'd taken her back to Kalifos and to his father, he'd turned his private army into Eleos. Mercy. Dedicated to saving people throughout the world, no matter what they needed. All because a little girl had given him hope and he'd wanted to pass that hope on to others.

Now that same little girl was giving him a pin crafted in her likeness. Giving him the gift of hope once again.

He'd never been one for signs or portents, and he'd never believed in fate. He'd never believed in anything much at all, but this gift of hers…it meant something. Hope for the future maybe, or perhaps something else, but it was something.

She stared at him now and he could see anxiety in her eyes, as if she was she worried he wouldn't like it. 'What do you mean, it's me?' she asked.

He ignored her for the moment, holding out

the box in her direction. 'Come here. Pin it on for me.' It came out sounding more like an order than anything else, but she came over to him and took the pin out of the box. Then she came in close and slid her fingers beneath his lapel, lifting it so she could pin the small Eleos symbol to his jacket.

He could smell her luscious scent, apples and musk, that never failed to get him hard, and could see the sparkle of a tear still caught on her golden lashes. His gift had meant something to her, too, something that had affected her every bit as deeply as hers had him.

Aristeidis's ring had seemed like the natural thing to give her since he'd been concerned she hadn't had an engagement ring. Why exactly he'd been concerned, he wasn't sure. He only knew that she'd wanted the trappings of a real wedding and if she wanted to organise them, he wasn't going to get in her way. Except it had bothered him that she hadn't had a ring and he didn't like the thought of her ordering one for herself.

He was the groom; it was his job to find one. So when he'd discovered Aristeidis's ring in amongst his father's belongings, knowing what his father had meant to her, it had seemed like the perfect ring for her. If she wanted something more feminine, he could get her something later.

But as soon as she'd seen it, it was clear to him that he wasn't going to need to get her another one. There had been tears in her eyes when he'd presented it to her, and that had made something shift inside himself too. A deep pleasure that he could do that for her, that he could give her something meaningful.

Perhaps that was why her gift to him had affected him so deeply. He'd already been moved by her reaction to the ring.

None of this should mean anything at all to you.

It was true, it shouldn't. Ever since that day when she'd got on her knees and made him lose control, he'd let her somehow get under his skin in a way he shouldn't have. He'd been thinking that he'd give himself a week, up until their marriage, to indulge himself, and then, after the wedding, he'd take himself back to Jamaica, find his detachment and his focus again. So perhaps it didn't matter if he let this be important to him now.

She finished with the pin, the platinum gleaming against the dark blue wool of his suit. It looked good there, a little reminder of the hope she'd always brought to him.

Her eyes were very dark as they looked up into his and he could see that she was still anxious. She wanted him to like this and it gave him a peculiar thrill to know his opinion mattered to her.

'Do you remember when I first saw you?' he asked. 'You were standing in the rubble and you had a knife in your hand. There were about five men who were going to attack you and you looked as if you could take on each and every one of them.'

A small crease appeared between her brows. 'Yes, I remember.'

'I fired my gun and they scattered. And I thought… I thought you'd run, too. But you didn't. You held your arms up to me instead.'

'I wasn't scared of you,' she said. 'I just… knew you were here to save me.'

Atticus touched the pin. 'This is you, Elena. That night I'd felt I'd come to a dead end. That I was no different from the men I was trying to protect people like you from. Then you appeared, and you seemed to see something in me that I'd thought had died a long time ago. You gave me hope. So when I started Eleos and I wanted a logo, all I could think about was you. You in the rubble, lifting your arms to me.'

Her eyes widened, a flush creeping over her skin. 'I… I had no idea. I didn't even realise you remembered that.'

'Of course, I remembered that.' Perhaps it had been a mistake to tell her what she represented to him, a ceding of power he hadn't been prepared for. Then again, if anyone should know the story behind the Eleos child, it should be her. She had been that child, after all.

Elena glanced at the pin then up at him once more. 'You like it?'

He put his hand over it, feeling the cool metal warm against his palm, and held her gaze, let her see what her gift had meant to him. 'Yes,' he said simply.

She smiled, so warm and sweet it stole his breath, and the glow that suffused her face made something inside him tighten.

You like making her smile.

And he wanted to do it again.

'I'm so glad,' she said, a little shyly. 'I love the ring too. Just before the will was read out I was hoping I'd get a few keepsakes from him. I thought you'd probably want the ring though.'

He hadn't known she'd actively been hoping for the ring. He'd just thought she might appreciate it.

You should tell her why you don't want anything from him. She deserves to know.

A cold thread wound through his pleasure. He'd been harsh when she'd asked him why he hadn't wanted anything of his father's, because harsh was his usual response when anyone asked him about Dorian. Harsh made sure no one ever questioned him again.

But…she knew already what had happened to his brother. It wasn't as if he was going to be telling her things she wasn't already aware of. Also, she was really the heir of the Kalathes fortune, not him, so why shouldn't she know the truth?

'You wanted to know why I didn't want anything of my father's?' The words came out roughly, but he didn't try to soften them. 'Because after Dorian died, he cut me off. Both emotionally and financially. He told me that he wished I had been the one to die, not Dorian. He told me that I had to leave Kalifos, and that he never wanted to see me again. I was sixteen.'

Shock then sympathy flickered over her face. 'Oh, Atticus…'

'So I left home and, since there was nothing else for me here, I joined the army. Over the years I tried periodically to make contact with him, but he always refused. He didn't want to talk to me and he didn't want to see me. He'd meant it when he said he never wanted to see me again.'

She'd gone pale, her eyes darkening. 'That was unforgivable of him,' she said quietly but with some force.

That surprised him. He'd expected her to come to Aristeidis's defence. 'He had reason,' Atticus said.

'He was wrong.' Her chin came up. 'He told me that he'd treated you badly and that he'd said some terrible things, but he was never clear on what exactly he'd said. He just didn't blame you for not wanting to see him.'

Unexpected grief twisted inside him. He didn't want to know about Aristeidis's regrets, especially when it was too late to do anything about them.

You let your own bitterness eat you alive the same way he let it eat at him.

Atticus gritted his teeth. Well, if he was bitter, didn't he have a right to it? The days, weeks, months and years after Dorian's death, he'd been suffering in his own private hell and had been desperate for someone to save him. Yet the one person who could had left him there to suffer instead.

Memories rose inside him, memories he'd been struggling to keep at bay while he'd been back here. Memories of his childhood here, with Dorian. Of playing chase in the villa and hide and seek in the gardens. Games of war with sticks for swords and the time he'd tied a towel around his neck as a cape and tried to jump from the window in this very room, thinking he could fly. Only for his brother to stop him, saving him...

A suffocating feeling rose inside him, the memories drowning him.

He had to get out of the room, go somewhere else. Perhaps to the pool or to run along the island's beaches. He needed fresh air, the scent of salt and the sea. He needed to push himself to exhaustion, needed the burn of his muscles as he pushed himself physically instead of the ache in his heart.

He went to turn, but then Elena reached out and gripped his arm. 'Wait.'

He could have pulled away, but somehow her touch eased the constriction in his chest so he stopped and glanced at her.

Her expression was full of painful sympathy. 'He was a good father to me,' she said. 'But he wasn't a good father to you, I can see that. He shouldn't have said all those terrible things to you. He should have been there for you, and I realise why you didn't want to talk to him.'

He hadn't known he'd needed her understanding until he saw it glowing in the depths of her eyes. 'Like I said. He had a right to it.'

'No,' Elena said quietly but very firmly. 'No, he didn't.'

How strange that it was he who now felt defensive of the man he'd felt nothing but bitter anger towards for the past twenty years.

'I killed my brother,' he said harshly. 'You don't think he had a right to be angry with me for that?'

'Not angrier than you were at yourself,' she said, as if she knew. As if she knew exactly what it was to be responsible for the death of another person. A person he'd loved. As if she knew exactly the depth of his bitterness and his self-loathing, because that was still there, deep down inside him.

A morass of pain and grief and fury and hatred.

At himself.

The sense of suffocation increased, making it feel as if there were hands around his throat, choking him. Abruptly he couldn't stand it.

He ripped his arm from her grip and strode out without a word.

CHAPTER EIGHT

ELENA STEPPED INTO the cool of the tiny Kalifos church that had only recently hosted Aristeidis's funeral and would now be hosting her wedding.

She adjusted her bouquet of calla lilies, while the woman she'd hired to help her dress, apply her make-up and do her hair fussed around with her gown.

She would have had a bridesmaid if she could, but growing up on Kalifos, which had isolated her anyway, and then looking after Aristeidis had left her little time for cultivating friendships. She could have done the make-up and hair herself, but she'd wanted to indulge herself on her wedding day, so she had.

After a few more twitches of her dress and a quick touch to her veil, the woman gave her a smile then disappeared through the door into the church, to tell Atticus that she'd arrived.

Elena took a couple of breaths to calm the twisting anxiety in her gut and to ease the tight band of emotion that had closed around her chest.

She wished Aristeidis were here. She wished her long-dead family were here. She wished she were marrying a man who loved her and whom she loved.

But none of that was to be. She was marrying Atticus to fulfil Aristeidis's last wish, and so she could stay in the home she loved, and to one day have the family of her own that she so longed for.

Not that you deserve to have that.

The doubt felt like a thorn sliding through her, but she ignored it, the way she always did. The wedding was happening and she would have all those other things too, irrespective of whether she deserved them or not. And she was grateful, that was what she was.

Her husband-to-be was beautiful and there was a lot of pleasure to be had in his bed. They hadn't discussed living arrangements or anything, but she'd assumed that once they were married he'd be living elsewhere, while she stayed on Kalifos. He'd clearly have to visit on occasion so she could conceive the children Aristeidis had specified, but he wouldn't otherwise impede her in any way. And she'd thought that she'd be happy with that.

Except…he was a difficult man, it was true, but she'd caught glimpses of another man beneath his hard shell. A man who'd dried her tears gently, then looked at her with shock and a fierce rush of emotion as he'd opened the box with the pin in it. Who'd then also given her a glimpse of the deep, sharp pain that lived inside him when he'd pulled his arm from her grip and had left the room so suddenly.

Behind the silk of her bodice, her heart ached. Both for the pain she'd seen in him and for the calm way he'd dried her tears. For how he'd put his hand over the pin she'd given him, as if he'd never had anything so precious, and told her that the symbol of Eleos was her.

She could still feel the echo of the shock that had caused her reverberating through her now. She'd had no idea that he'd even remembered the day he'd found her, let alone that she'd changed something in him. That she had been the reason he'd started his charity.

She'd had no idea that she'd represented hope for him.

The ache in her heart deepened into a bittersweet pain. Bitter that he'd been so despairing and yet so sweet that she'd helped him. She'd never helped anyone except Aristeidis before, and it mattered to her that the person she'd helped had been him. That she'd given him hope when he'd had none.

You can't let this—him—mean anything to you.

She shouldn't. He'd already told her that love wouldn't be a part of this marriage, so getting further involved with him, letting him mean something to her, letting herself be vulnerable to him, would only be setting herself up for further pain.

But…he was clearly still tormented by the death of his brother—the brief flash of pain and rage in his eyes before he'd walked out the night before had been clear evidence of that—and that made her hurt for him. That made her want to help him, too.

Aristeidis had told her what had happened to Dorian, and he'd also told Elena that he 'hadn't handled it well'. An understatement, apparently.

The death of Dorian had fractured an already tenuous relationship, Aristeidis letting grief overwhelm him, causing him to alienate his youngest son, piling more salt onto what was already an open wound.

Atticus blamed himself for his brother's death, that was obvious. He was already angry and his father had made things worse by blaming him too. Instead of helping them both grieve, Aristeidis had broken their relationship entirely. And he'd regretted it deeply.

She'd helped him with his regrets, but it had been he who'd decided that he needed to talk to Atticus. To try and rebuild what he'd broken.

Too late.

The music was starting, signalling her entrance, but she had to take another moment as yet more tears prickled, making her have to blink hard so they wouldn't ruin her make-up.

Well, Aristeidis had gone, but his son was still here and she was going to marry him. He'd given her a glimpse of the pain that lay in his heart and maybe he wouldn't reveal more. Or maybe that was the start. But she wanted to help him, maybe rebuild the relationship that Aristeidis had destroyed. That was the least she could do, surely?

Decision made, Elena gripped her flowers tightly as the doors were pulled open. Then she walked down the aisle of Kalifos's small, ancient stone church, smelling of incense and old stone, hand-carved wooden pews on either side of her.

At the other end of the aisle, Atticus waited.

He wore a morning suit of dove grey, with a crisp white shirt that emphasised his tanned skin and the darkness of his eyes. The pure planes and angles of his face were set in hard lines, yet the moment his gaze settled on her, something fierce and hot leapt in it.

A wave of heat washed over her as he took in her dress and the veil that covered her hair and face, the flames in his eyes leaping higher. It was very, very clear he liked her wedding gown.

She took a little breath, unable to help noticing that in place of flowers on his lapel, he had the pin she'd given him the night before. It gleamed softly in the dim light.

He was so beautiful.

You can't fall for him. He'll never give you what you want.

Good thing that she wasn't falling for him then. He made her ache, but it wasn't with longing. It was sympathy for what he'd gone through, for the pain he still felt for his brother's death, and for the fact that his father had died and there would never be a reconciliation for either of them.

It wasn't for herself and some old longing that she'd put behind her years ago, the longing of a child for someone to protect her, someone to trust, someone to love. Because she couldn't love him. He'd left her, he'd abandoned her all those years ago and, while she knew he'd had to, she couldn't trust that he wouldn't do so again. Especially when there was nothing tying him to her but the last wish of a dying man.

She would never allow herself to be so vulnerable to him again.

Elena finally came to a stop at the altar, her heartbeat thumping in her chest, nerves gathering inside her despite the fact that this was simply a legal procedure. It didn't mean anything.

Atticus was still staring at her as if he

couldn't look away, and somehow it made her nerves both worse and better. Then he frowned slightly and held out his hand to her and automatically she took it. His fingers curled around hers, warm and strong, and abruptly the flutter inside her settled. Relieved, she gave him an instinctive smile through her veil and her nerves settled even further when he smiled back.

You should be worried, not calmed.

Elena ignored the thought as the priest began the ceremony and when it came time to say her vows, she was able to speak levelly and without a stutter or nervous tremble. Atticus said his too, his deep, dark voice as calm as hers, though there was nothing calm in the look he gave her. It just about burned her to the ground.

He kept holding her hand throughout, the warmth of his touch soothing, yet at the exchange of rings she could feel the electric shock that crackled over her skin as he slid the wedding band onto her finger. Then it was her turn, his large hand in hers, the white scars on his fingers standing out against his skin as she did the same with his ring.

Then the priest pronounced them husband

and wife and Atticus was lifting her veil and putting it back. There was an intense light in his eyes, some strange emotion glowing there that she didn't understand. It was sexual heat, she was familiar enough with that by now to recognise it, but there was also something else there, something deeper.

He took her chin in his hand the way he had the night before, his touch just as gentle, and tilted her head back. For a moment he said nothing, only looked at her as if she were a prize that he'd worked long and hard for and had now won. It made her own heart twist, full of the same longing she'd already told her herself she didn't feel. And then she had no more time to think, because he bent his head and kissed her. His mouth was hot, yet unexpectedly gentle and his kiss was sweet, deepening the ache in her heart.

How much sweeter all of this would be if they loved each other, if they'd chosen each other. If their future were a life spent together and the family they'd create.

You can't want more, not with him, and you know it.

Yes, she did. If she was ever to have the future she really wanted for herself, she wouldn't have it with him. She could *never* have it with him.

Elena was shaking a little by the time he lifted his mouth, the fierce expression still burning in his eyes. And abruptly she wanted to know what it was that made him look at her that way. She wanted to know what he was feeling and whether this was as emotionally complicated for him as it was for her. Whether this mattered to him and whether the future he'd envisioned for himself featured her in any way.

She knew she shouldn't be thinking things like that, but she couldn't help herself. Even though they'd been sleeping together for the past week, he was still a stranger to her, despite all the stories she'd heard about him, and despite her knowing the tragedy that had shaped him. Yet those stories had been about the boy he'd once been, not the man, and it was the man who was her husband now. It was the man she wanted to know more about.

And why not? Five years, Aristeidis had stipulated, that was how long they were supposed to be together, so why couldn't they have some kind of relationship during that time? They would be lovers, yes, but why not friends too? She should know more about the father of her children, she really should.

Atticus threaded his fingers through hers and then she was being led out of the church and onto the bright sunlight.

She'd organised for their honeymoon to be in a villa along the Adriatic coast in Italy, and a helicopter would take them to Athens and to the Kalathes jet that would then take them to Italy. Atticus had agreed to it all without question when she'd told him about it and she was already planning in her head the questions she was going to ask him once they'd got there, when he said, 'I have cancelled the Italy trip.'

They were walking up the small rocky path that led from the church back to the Kalathes villa, and she stopped in shock, her veil flying out behind her as the wind caught it.

'What?'

He'd stopped too, the burning look that he'd given her back in the church in his eyes once again. 'We will not be going to Italy. I've decided we'll be going to Jamaica instead.'

Elena stood there in the bright sunlight, the crystals in her wedding gown glittering, her veil fluttering out behind her like a flag, her eyes dark and smoky. Her golden hair was in a beautiful arrangement on top of her head, all soft curls and threaded through with wild-flowers. There were lilies in her hand and on the other hand glowed his father's ring. His wedding band was there too, the wedding band she'd designed.

She was so beautiful it almost hurt to look at her.

Your wife. She's your wife now.

Being here on Kalifos, where he'd grown up, had triggered memories he didn't want, memories he'd been trying to escape. He'd been plagued by them the past week, and even up until last night all he'd been able to think about were all the moments his brother had missed, all the firsts Dorian would never have. He'd never marry, for example. He'd never get to see his bride standing in the sun, sparkling like a fall of stardust.

It should have been you who died and it should be him standing here now, looking at Elena.

It should, but it wasn't, and normally that would feel like a knife sliding directly into his heart. Yet all he felt now was a savage satisfaction that it *wasn't* Dorian standing here, looking at Elena. That it was *him* instead.

You don't deserve this.

No, of course he didn't. But he wasn't going to turn away from it either and he'd realised that the moment the music had started and the church doors had opened, and Elena had appeared, glowing like an angel fallen to earth.

He'd spent all night trying and failing to forget about the discussion they'd had about Dorian. Trying and failing to forget about the understanding he'd seen in her eyes and how she'd told him that his father had been too hard on him. How she'd seemed to know about the anger that lived in his heart. The anger at himself that he couldn't seem to outrun.

He'd never known what to do with that anger except bury it so far down he forgot it was there, and he didn't know what to do with her understanding either. It felt dangerous, though he couldn't have said why, so he'd spent the entire morning as he'd prepared for their wedding battling to find his usual detachment, his usual focus, pushing all the thoughts of the past to one side.

Until she'd walked down the aisle towards

him. And he'd realised that all his attempts at detachment, his burying of the tragedy of Dorian's death, were useless. He couldn't outrun the past or the memories. He couldn't bury those terrible, painful emotions, just as he couldn't bury or outrun his intense desire for her.

She made it impossible. Because right from the first moment he'd seen her, she'd brought all his bitter emotions to the surface. She'd brought them out into the open and then she'd eased them.

She was his hope. That was why he'd rescued her from the rubble and given her to his father to look after. That was why he'd started Eleos. That was why millions of people now had better lives and it was all because of her.

She was his hope for the future, his hope of redemption. His hope of healing. She'd given him that pin and now she was giving him herself, and he knew he couldn't refuse her.

He hadn't given much thought to what form their marriage would take, half thinking that he'd live in Jamaica while she lived on Kalifos, and every six months or so he'd visit her to conceive the children his father had specified. There had been no stipulation, after all, that they were to live as husband and wife.

But as she'd walked down the aisle to him in that church and the realisation had hit him of what she was to him, of what she represented, he'd changed his mind. They *would* live together as husband and wife, and he'd be her husband in all ways. He'd be a father to her children. He'd give her the family she'd always wanted.

Love was still out of the question, but he could make her happy without it, he was sure. No, he *would* make her happy. She was the hope he clung to and, because of that, he couldn't let her go. He wouldn't. There would be no hope at all if he did.

They'd need to discuss where they'd live, naturally, since he didn't want to be on Kalifos, but perhaps she'd like his island in Jamaica. Or perhaps they'd find somewhere else. Either way, she was his now.

She'd changed his life all those years ago, and now she was changing it again. She was giving him back the hope he'd lost and he couldn't turn away from it, not again.

She's more than just a representation

of hope. She's also a woman with her own dreams and needs.

Well, of course she was, and he'd treat her as such. He wasn't that much of a monster.

'Jamaica?' she repeated blankly.

Of course, Jamaica for the honeymoon. It made sense. He wanted to bring her back to the island that meant something to him. He'd kept himself alone and apart from people for so long, but he didn't need to with her. She already knew the worst parts of him and he was done with hiding them.

'Italy is beautiful,' he said. 'But my island is home to me. More of a home than Kalifos. And I'd like to show it to you, spend some time with you there.'

The shock vanished from her face, her brown eyes glowing. 'Oh, yes,' she breathed, as if she couldn't think of anything better. 'Yes, I'd love to go in that case.'

Satisfaction gripped him, along with a rush of intense desire at the obvious delight on her face. He'd expected her to argue about the sudden change of plans, not look thrilled at the thought of returning to a place she'd already been. 'Good. It's a bit of a trek, so I've organised for us to leave tomorrow. Tonight, though…' he gripped her hand, pulling her gently but firmly close '…it's our wedding night and I want to make sure it's one you won't forget.'

Colour swept through her cheeks, which he found adorable. It made him bend to kiss her, a light brush of his lips against hers that only incited him further. Impatient, he stepped back and turned, pulling her along with him up the path to the villa.

As they reached the entrance, he swept her up into his arms and carried her over the threshold, and he knew she loved the gesture, because her eyes sparkled and she smiled, her head back against his shoulder.

He didn't take her to the master bedroom, or to the bedroom that he'd once had as a child. He didn't take her to the guest room he'd been using either; there were too many memories associated with all of them. Her room, though, the only memories he had of it were of pleasure.

It overlooked the sea and a white terrace, and best of all the bed was big and wide, covered in a thick white quilt and blue cushions.

He set her down in the middle of the room and pulled the veil from her hair, before carefully laying it out on the couch near the window. Then he took her by the shoulders and turned her around so he could undo the many tiny buttons on the back of her dress.

As the heavy fabric fell away, it revealed pale, silky skin. She wore nothing underneath her gown except a pair of lacy knickers and high-heeled sandals.

Desire gripped him, his satisfaction deepening, and he let it run through him, sharpening his hunger to a fine point. She was his wife. She was *his* and he'd never had anyone of his own before. He hadn't known how deeply that would matter to him.

The male beast in him wanted to gorge itself on her as soon as possible, but he'd already decided he wasn't going to rush it. This was her wedding night and she was his wife, and savouring her was no less than she deserved.

She had given him hope and so he would give her pleasure.

He helped her to step out of her dress and then he laid that out over the couch too, before coming back to her. She'd gone the prettiest shade of pink, the wildflowers still woven in her lovely hair.

This time it was his turn to kneel, he decided, and he did so before her, lifting his hands to run them up her thighs, stroking the warm satin of her skin, and making her tremble. Her eyes were dark and smoky as she looked down at him, and he held her gaze as he hooked his fingers into the lace of her underwear, slowly drawing it down. She swallowed, the pulse at the base of her throat beating fast, her cheeks flushed.

He helped her step out of the lacy fabric and then got rid of it, so that all she wore were her high-heeled sandals and nothing else.

She was the most beautiful thing he'd ever seen in his life.

Another moment Dorian will never get to have: a wedding night.

The thought was a knife, cutting him open, but he shoved it aside. He wasn't going to think about his brother, not now, not here. This was for him. *She* was for him. She was his hope and he had to believe in the future she represented. He had to.

He ran his hands up her thighs again, leaning in and pressing kisses against her stomach, stroking her softly rounded curves, filling himself with her delicious, sweet and musky scent. She was getting aroused now, he could smell it, so he explored lower, nuzzling against the soft curls between her thighs.

She shivered in his hands, a sound escaping her as he kissed down to the sweet heat that lay between her legs. He leaned in further, tasting her with his tongue, filling his hands with softness of her rear and squeezing gently as he held her still for his mouth. He pushed his tongue inside her, tasting her deeper, licking her and making her gasp. Her fingers were in his hair, twisting, gripping him tightly as he gorged himself on her flavour and the way she shivered and gasped against him.

He brought her to climax quickly and hard, and she cried his name, sagging against him as if she couldn't hold herself upright any longer. He rose to his feet, picking her up in his arms and taking her to the bed. Then he put her down on the mattress and with slow care removed her sandals. He took his time, undoing the strap of each one, cradling her small foot as he slipped them off.

She lay back on the white sheets, her skin beautifully flushed, her hair a golden veil across the pillows with wildflowers scattered everywhere, her eyes glowing like banked coals from the pleasure he'd just given her. There was pleasure in this too, in taking her shoes off, in stroking her feet and making her giggle and squirm.

That made him smile, which surprised him. He couldn't remember the last time he'd smiled during sex. He couldn't remember the last time he'd smiled at all, at least not when it hadn't been at her.

And then her shoes were off and his clothes felt too tight. He wanted her bare skin against his, and so he clawed them off, discarding them carelessly on the floor before joining her on the bed. He moved over her, settling himself between her thighs and lowering his head to kiss her, deep and hot. Letting her taste herself on him.

She gave a soft, throaty moan, her hips lifting against his in blatant demand. But he was still taking his time, so he teased them both, rubbing the hard length of his shaft against the tender flesh of her sex, making her gasp and clutch at him. But soon he too lost patience, easing her thighs wide and pushing inside her in a long, slow, deep glide.

'Atticus…' Her back arched, her eyes gone

liquid and dark as the night sky. She felt so good around him, tight and wet and so hot his brain momentarily blanked.

She was beneath him, taking all of him, looking up at him as if he was the best thing she'd seen all day. As if he was the best thing she'd ever seen in her entire life.

No one had ever looked at him like that. No one.

Then she lifted her arms to him the way she had all those years ago, her hands on his shoulders, gripping him as if she never wanted to let him go, and he began to move inside her, deep and slow.

Pleasure was a dark pulse inside him, so strong and getting stronger, and he could see it reflected in her eyes too. Her nails dug into him and she didn't look away. 'Atticus,' she whispered as he slid his hands beneath her, lifting her hips so he could move deeper. 'Oh, my God…'

She was electric around him, fierce ecstasy arcing through him and spitting sparks, the trail of a comet flying in a night sky.

'Elena.' He could taste her name. It had a flavour all its own and that was something else he wanted to savour. 'My Elenitsa.'

She shuddered, staring up at him as he moved inside her, fast and getting faster, twisting everything tight and making it desperate. Her legs closed around his waist, her hips moving with his, falling into his rhythm as if born to it.

There was ecstasy between them, a fever that grew with every thrust of his hips, and he had one moment's fleeting doubt that he was perhaps feeling all this a lot more strongly than he should have, when it all exploded in a wild flame, and he let them both burn until they were nothing but sparks and ash on the wind.

CHAPTER NINE

'THIS IS VERY UNFAIR,' Elena protested. 'Let me see.' Atticus had his hands over her eyes and she couldn't see a thing. It was very annoying.

'It's a surprise,' he said from behind her, guiding her across sand still warm from the day's sun. 'And if I let you see, it would spoil the surprise.'

She sighed. 'Your logic is both irrefutable and deeply irritating.'

'I know.' He finally stopped and took his hands away. 'You can look now.'

Elena blinked as her eyes adjusted.

It was night, the sky above studded with stars, but in front of her, set on a platform of smooth inlaid rock that faced the beach, was a big white porcelain claw-foot bath. A rock wall sat behind the bath, the taps inset into it, and small tea lights in coloured glass holders had been placed on ledges that looked custom made for that purpose. The flames leapt and flickered and danced, casting shadows everywhere. Around the bath were small trees to give a bit of privacy, and they had been strung with small solar fairy lights, bathing everything in a warm glow. The bath itself was full of gently steaming water, and there were even petals floating in it.

Atticus had said he'd prepared a surprise for her early that afternoon, but she'd never guessed it would be an outdoor bath. They'd been here a few days already and she hadn't even known it was there.

Then again, they hadn't ventured much beyond the house, too busy with exploring each other, let alone the island. He had taken her out fishing earlier that day, showing her the rocks in the lagoon and the best places to cast a line. She'd loved it and had been especially excited when she'd caught a fish of her own. He'd prepared it and cooked it for her for dinner that night, and it had been delicious.

In fact, everything about being here with him was delicious, from the long, lazy mornings in bed, to a swim in the clear waters of the lagoon, and lunch in the deck facing the sea. Then usually some more lazy, sun-drenched sex on the deck or on the sand, or in the water, depending on when and where they were at the time, before dinner, that Atticus insisted on preparing himself.

He was also a joy to be with. As soon as they'd arrived it was as if a heavy weight had lifted from him. He was still intense and sharp and focused, but there was an easiness to him, as if something coiled tight inside him had relaxed. He smiled. He laughed. He teased her as if they'd known each other for years, grinning as she teased him back.

He asked her what she'd been doing over the years, listening to her speak as if he'd never heard anything more important in his life. Then he told her about his own past, stories from his days in the army and then as a mercenary in his own private security force. She found it fascinating. She found *him* fascinating, everything about him, and she hadn't expected that. Sex and as much pleasure as she could handle, yes. But talking deep into the night with Atticus about Eleos and his mission to save as many people as he could? Telling him about the intricacies and challenges of Kalathes Shipping? Giggling like a schoolgirl as he tickled her feet and then laughing as she poked him in the sides, trying to find out where he was ticklish? No. Not at all.

And then there was how he did everything for her, waiting on her hand and foot, ignoring her completely when she told him she wasn't helpless and that she could do some things herself. She didn't mind. After the years of caring for Aristeidis, she secretly loved having someone take care of her for a change.

Tomorrow, he'd promised they'd go snorkelling in the lagoon and then he'd take out the yacht and he'd teach her to sail. And maybe the day after that they'd go into Port Antonio so she could look around and maybe get dinner there.

She loved it. She loved him showing her around the island, taking her to all his favourite places, showing her pieces of himself that no one else knew. He was such a caring man, the evidence not just in how he believed totally in his charity and his mission, but also in how he treated with care the nature he lived in. He showed her how he collected rainwater for the house and recycled the grey water. How he used solar power for everything, collecting sun the way he collected the rain. He showed her the garden where he grew herbs and other greens. He showed her the office where he ran his charity, linked to the rest of the world from this peaceful, quiet place by satellites.

Several times she wondered why he'd taken himself away from society quite so completely, when it was apparent from his visit to Greece that he had no problems actually being around people. She wanted to ask him, but the moment was never quite right. She was loving being with him like this and she didn't want to destroy the mood with questions that he wouldn't want to answer.

You wanted to help him find his way back to his father.

She did, but as she stared at the outdoor bath, at the dancing tea lights and the stack of towels on the stone pad, she knew that this was another moment she didn't want to destroy with questions.

Instead, she turned to him with shining eyes. 'I love it. It's amazing.'

He smiled, the flickering flames of the tea lights and the fairy lights overhead casting shadows over his beautiful face and the hard, carved lines of his body. They were both naked and she'd become used to wandering around the island either wearing nothing or merely a light wrap. There was no one to see them and it was too hot for clothes most of the time.

'Get in,' he said. 'The water's warm.'

So she did, delighted when he got in too, sitting behind her so that she could settle back in his arms, the warm water lapping around them. The night was quiet as most of the nights here were, the only sound the waves on the beach and the wind in the palms.

'I want to talk to you about our future,' Atticus said unexpectedly as she felt him pour water over her hair.

She tried not to tense. The future was an unwelcome subject and one she'd been deliberately not thinking about for the past three days, wanting to enjoy the moments she had with him. She knew eventually they'd have to decide what their future would look like and she was pretty sure it would be apart. And she didn't like the little lurch in her heart the prospect of that gave her. She was supposed to enjoy her honeymoon and then equally enjoy living on her own on Kalifos.

She wasn't supposed to feel a sharp pang of loss at the thought of leaving him.

'Oh?' she asked, hoping it sounded casual and not as tense as she felt.

Behind her he turned, reaching over the side of the bath for the bottle of shampoo that stood on a small stool. He put some in his hands and then began lathering her hair. It felt soothing. Over the past couple of days, she'd learned he wasn't a man who liked to sit still. He always had to be doing something with his hands. She liked that too since what he did with his hands was either something interesting or intensely pleasurable for her.

A deep, animal pleasure stole the tension from her now as those hands moved in her hair and she relaxed back against him.

'I think we should live together,' he said. 'As husband and wife. It can either be here or somewhere else, I don't mind where as long as it's not Kalifos.'

Elena's muscles locked up in shock. She had *not* expected that he'd want them to live together, especially when he'd been so clear that their marriage was merely for Aristeidis's will.

'Why?' she asked blankly. 'I thought that—'

'I know, but I've changed my mind.' He eased her back further against him, then urged her deeper into the water so her hair was submerged. She found herself looking up at him, his black eyes holding hers, the same ferocious expression in them as there'd been the day of their wedding. 'I want us to have a real marriage,' he went on. 'To have a family together. Bring up our children together.'

A shiver went through her. He began squeezing out her hair, rinsing away the shampoo, and she couldn't stop staring up at him.

A real marriage. Having a family with him. Living with him as his wife...

Her heart ached with a longing she'd tried to ignore for a long time now. The longing to be with someone, to have someone of her own, someone who wouldn't leave her.

It can't be him. It can't.

A thread of panic wound through her, making her feel as if she'd made a mistake somewhere along the line, a mistake that it was now too late to fix.

She sat up abruptly, water streaming from her hair, her back to him. She didn't want to look at him, didn't want him to see her panic. The water was warm but she felt cold. 'I see,' she said, trying to sound as neutral as possible. 'What made you change your mind?'

If he'd picked up on her tension he gave no sign, his hands in her hair again, squeezing the water from it gently. 'You did,' he said. 'The day of our wedding. Or maybe it was even the night before, when you gave me that pin.'

Her heart thumped loudly in her ears and she was suddenly full of fear though, again, she wasn't sure why. She leaned forward in the water, wrapping her arms around her knees. 'How did I do that?'

'I told you that the night I found you in the rubble, you gave me hope.' His voice was a deep rumble at her back. 'And when you gave me that pin, I was reminded of it. Then in the church, when you appeared in your wedding gown, it was as if you were giving me yourself. You've always been hope to me, Elenitsa, and on our wedding day, you gave me hope again.' His hands stroked down her spine and she shivered helplessly. 'Hope for a future I didn't know I wanted. A future I thought I couldn't have.'

His words made her heart clench. They

should make her feel good, she knew, because who didn't want to be someone's hope? But there was only a kind of lurching disappointment. This wasn't about her. This wasn't about who she was. It was about what she represented to him. Of course, she liked being his hope, but...

You want to be more than that to him.

Her feelings tangled and knotted inside her, cold fear and disappointment, that terrible aching longing and a sharp kind of sadness. No, she hadn't wanted to be more to him, she hadn't wanted him to matter to her at all, and yet... Part of her knew the truth. That he did matter to her. That the past three days with him had been the happiest of her life, happier than she'd ever been as Aristeidis's daughter.

You're falling for him.

No, no. No, she couldn't do that. The was the very last thing in the world that she should do.

Too late.

Elena gripped the side of the bath tightly, the cold fear inside her winding deeper. 'Oh,' she said, sharper than she'd intended. 'So it's not really about me, then?' As soon as the words were out of her mouth, she knew she shouldn't have said them. They revealed far too much. But like most things to do with Atticus, it was too late.

He'd gone still behind her. 'What do you mean?'

'I mean, you don't really want to live with me.'

'Of course I want to live with you.' There was a puzzled note in his voice. 'Wasn't that what I just said?'

She turned her head, glancing at him from over her shoulder. 'You said you wanted to live with me because of what I represent. That's not about me, Atticus. That's about you.'

His black brows drew down, the flames from the tea lights leaping in his night-dark eyes. 'It's you I want to live with, Elena. Is that not clear?'

'No, it's not clear. You said I represented hope for you. Hope is what you want to live with, it's not me.' Her throat had tightened. She didn't want to argue with him, but it felt as if the conversation had got away from her and she didn't know how to get it back.

His gaze became edged, focusing on her

in that abrupt way he had that made her feel as if he could read every thought in her head.

He'll know how you feel about him. He'll be able to see it.

The thread of panic constricted and abruptly she didn't want to be here any longer, in the warm water with him and his seductive hands and his sharp gaze. She felt far too vulnerable, far too open, and she hated it. She'd always hated it.

He'll know about how you left them, too. He'll know what a coward you are.

The water surged as Elena pushed herself up and out of the bath, splashing onto the stone pad.

'Elena?' Atticus sounded shocked. 'Elena, what is it?'

But she didn't answer. She felt cold, the kind of chill that had nothing to do with the temperature, and she had to get away from him. She couldn't be around him a second longer. Picking up a towel, she wrapped it around herself, then stalked back into the house without a word.

Atticus sat for a moment in the bath, staring after her. He had no idea what had happened, but something had upset her. And she was upset, that was obvious. He'd thought she'd enjoy the outdoor bath and she certainly had been doing before he'd mentioned living together as husband and wife.

He'd been planning on having the conversation since they'd arrived on the island, but he'd thought he'd give them both a few days to get comfortable with each other, and to take the edge off the seemingly bottomless well of desire he had for her.

He'd thought to surprise her with the bath since she was such a sensual creature, and he knew she'd enjoy it. Then he'd bring the subject up when she was relaxed and in his arms. He hadn't thought it would be a big deal, especially not given the past couple of days.

Being with her had been a revelation. She'd fallen into the rhythms of the island as if born to them, seemingly delighted by everything he showed her. She was up for anything he suggested, even demanding that he show her how to fillet and prepare the fish she caught. She was fascinated by how he recycled everything he could because he wanted to leave as minimal a footprint on the island as possible, which had then led to a discussion about sustainable housing, which was something he wanted to develop with Eleos.

She was so interesting. She had a quick mind and could see the big picture in a way that he sometimes struggled with, since he was so detail oriented. She also had the sweetest laugh that he soon found himself obsessed with, and coaxing her glorious smile out made him feel as if he'd won a gold medal.

He wanted more of that and his suggestion of them living together was merely a natural extension of what they were already doing. So what was it about it that she hadn't liked? Did it really matter why he wanted them to live together? She'd seemed upset about him calling her his hope, that it meant it wasn't really her that he wanted, and clearly that mattered to her. But why? What more did she want from him? They'd married for the will, that was all, but surely that didn't mean they couldn't live together or raise a family together. He wanted that and he knew that she wanted it too, so what was the issue?

Annoyance collected inside him. He hadn't handled this well, it was clear, otherwise she wouldn't have walked off, but if she thought he'd leave it at that, she was mistaken. This was important, their future was important, and he wanted it sorted out sooner rather than later.

Getting out of the bath, Atticus gave himself a cursory dry-off with a towel and then strode back along the path and into the house.

He found Elena in the bedroom, in the process of belting a long silk robe of blue Chinese silk very firmly around her. It annoyed him unreasonably.

He'd loved how she'd become so comfortable with him and with herself that she wasn't bothered that they didn't wear clothes most of the day. It was a far cry from the prissy cream suit she'd worn the first day she'd come here and he'd dumped her in the ocean.

But now the fact that she wore a robe, covering up her beautiful body, felt as if she was putting distance between them. As if she was armouring herself, and he didn't like that, not at all.

'What's wrong?' he asked, trying not to make it sound like a demand. 'Why are you upset?'

Her expression was very set and she half turned away from him, squeezing her hair out with the towel she had wrapped around it. 'It's nothing,' she said dismissively. 'Forget it.'

She was lying through her teeth and that annoyed him as well. He was tempted to provoke her into an argument, since they sparked so completely off each other that it would likely end up in bed. She'd probably forget all about whatever was upsetting her then, so maybe it would be worth it.

This will take more than just sex and you know it.

Doubt shifted inside him and an odd desperation he didn't know what to do with. This had to be discussed, whatever it was, because he had the sense that if it wasn't, the future he wanted with her would slip through his fingers. He couldn't have that; he just couldn't.

'No,' he said flatly. 'I'm not going to forget it. Tell me what's wrong.'

She squeezed the towel one more time then dropped it, her hair falling around her shoulders in damp, pretty golden curls. Her eyes were very dark and he could see pain glittering in them. 'I told you what was wrong. You say I'm your hope, Atticus, but I'm not. I'm your wife. I'm a person, not a…a talisman.'

A flicker of surprise cut through his anger

and frustration. He didn't see her that way. How could she think that? After the past few days?

Don't you? Isn't that exactly how you see her? How you've always seen her?

'What makes you think that?' he demanded, ignoring the thought.

'You said I was your hope for the future.' Her chin came up, her dark eyes full of anger. 'That's not about me, is it? That's all about you, Atticus.'

Something in his chest twisted hard. 'It's not about me,' he snapped before he could stop himself. 'It's about Dorian.'

Her gaze flickered, her expression softening. 'What about Dorian?'

He didn't want to talk about this—he never wanted to talk about this—but back in Greece he'd decided he couldn't outrun the past. And that she was the one person in this world who knew all about the tragedy that had taken Dorian's life. He didn't have to explain it to her. Yet still, the words were hard to find.

'He…will never have this,' Atticus said roughly. 'He will never have a wife and he'll never have a family. And so since I have the opportunity, I…owe it to him to have both.'

Pain flickered in Elena's eyes for a moment, then her lashes lowered, veiling her gaze. 'I see. So this future you want, this life you're planning on, is for him, not for you.' It wasn't a question.

There was a heavy sensation in his chest as if a boulder had fallen on him and he were lying pinned beneath it, struggling to get a breath. 'It's not just for him. Elena, I… I haven't seen a future for me, not one that includes a wife and children. But… I told you, Aristeidis's will, marrying you, it was as if fate was trying to tell me something. That perhaps I deserved after all to have the things that I took from Dorian.'

She stared at him for a long moment, her brown eyes soft with an emotion he didn't understand, sympathy almost and a terrible kind of understanding. Terrible, because it hurt, as if she'd slid a sharp knife between his ribs. 'You think you don't deserve those things?' she asked.

The harsh laugh escaped him before he could stop it. 'Of course I don't deserve them. I killed my own brother. Why would I deserve anything of the kind?'

'Atticus…' She took a step towards him

then stopped. 'It was an accident. You were very young and—'

'I still killed him,' he interrupted roughly. 'Yes, I was young. But I was unfamiliar with the gun he gave me and I didn't bother to listen to his safety instructions, because I was excited. Because I wanted to go hunting with my big brother.' It felt as if his heart were full of ground glass, every beat causing him agony, but he made himself go on, because now he'd started he couldn't seem to shut himself up. But she had to know. She had to know the ugly truth.

'We saw a deer and Dorian told me to wait while he got a bit closer. But I couldn't wait. I was impatient and excited and nervous. I wanted to prove myself to him. There was a movement in the trees and I pulled the trigger thinking it was the deer.' The beat of his heart was so full of agony, it would never be any less painful, never. 'But it wasn't the deer. It was Dorian.' And just like that, he was back in the dusty hills, surrounded by brush and short scrubby trees, suffocating in horror when he'd discovered what he'd done…

'Atticus.' Soft hands cupped his face. 'Atticus, come back to me.'

He blinked at the sound of his name, his heart racing, for a moment still lost in the horror of it all. Then his vision cleared, and instead of Dorian's wide unseeing gaze, it was Elena's warm brown eyes looking at him, full of concern. 'You're here,' she said softly. 'You're here on the island with me.'

He felt cold, as if he'd been plunged into a snow drift. 'Baba blamed me,' he said hoarsely. 'He was right to. I pulled that trigger, no one else. Dorian was the oldest. He should have lived, not me. But... Aristeidis was my father and he should have helped me. I needed him and he left me to suffer.'

Elena's arms were around him, all the soft warmth of her body pressed to his, surrounding him in her scent, and for a second all he could do was stand there trying to hold onto the present while all the past wanted to do was drag him down and suck him under.

When he was in despair, she always seemed to be there when he needed her, holding him.

But what have you done for her? Nothing.

He shoved the thought away, because he had too much weighing him down already. He didn't need anything more. Instead he concentrated on her and her heat, grounding him in the here and now.

Her hair was silky against his skin, her face pressed to his chest, her arms holding him tight. 'I'm sorry,' she said in a muffled voice, threaded through with pain. 'I'm so sorry, Atticus.'

'Sorry?' he repeated blankly. 'Sorry for what?'

She lifted her head and looked up at him, her eyes darkened, and he could see the gleam of tears on her cheeks. 'For what you went through. And for what your father put you through too. You didn't deserve that. You *didn't*.' Her gaze turned fierce. 'It *was* an accident, Atticus. But you can't keep blaming yourself for it for ever. You can't keep torturing yourself, either. There comes a point where you have to let it go.'

He lifted a hand, touched one of the tears on her cheeks. Tears she'd cried for him. 'Does there come a point? Tell me, have you been able to let go your tragedies?'

He'd never asked her about her family and she'd never spoken about them. When he'd rescued her, she'd been a traumatised child and he hadn't wanted to visit more pain on her by questioning her. And it seemed, despite what she'd told him about letting go and despite all the years that had passed, that pain still lived inside her.

She glanced away, golden lashes veiling her gaze. 'I… I'm trying to.'

He let his fingers trail down her cheek to her jaw and then along to her chin where he gripped it gently. 'Your family, hmm?'

She kept her gaze averted but didn't pull away. 'I had to let them go. I had to let them lie in the rubble of my home. Because if I kept them with me, I'd never have been able to settle into Kalifos. I would never have been able to connect with Aristeidis. I would have been constantly wishing for something I could never have again, and there's no point in that.'

But there was an uncertain note in her voice, as if she didn't believe what she was saying herself. 'And did you do that, Elenitsa?' he asked, allowing himself to be distracted from his own pain so he could concentrate on hers. 'Were you able to leave them in the past?'

Her throat moved and, to his shock, more tears seeped from beneath her lashes. 'After the earthquake, I woke up to find myself surrounded by rubble. I was alone. I thought… I thought I could hear my father shouting. I thought he was still alive. I tried to get to him, but there were people yelling and screaming and the aftershocks… I was so afraid. I ran and hid in the ruins.' Another tear slid down her cheek. 'There were rescue workers helping dig through the rubble to find survivors, and I tried to tell them about my family, but they were so busy. They didn't listen to me and I was so terrified I ran and hid again.'

His heart contracted at the hurt in her voice, a dull ache in his chest, and he stroked her chin gently, wanting to soothe her however he could.

'I shouldn't have left them,' she went on, her voice raw. 'I should have tried harder to get help. They might have been alive and they might have—'

'No,' he interrupted, appalled that she'd been carrying this pain and doubt around with her for so long, and clearly torturing herself with it too. He was appalled at himself as well, because he could have given her this relief years ago and he hadn't thought of it. He'd left her alone instead. 'No, Elena.'

Her lashes lifted slowly, her dark eyes meeting his.

'Your family died instantly,' he went on. 'I checked. I made sure. You couldn't have saved them even if you'd managed to get the rescue teams to search through the rubble. You didn't leave them, sweetheart. They were already gone.'

She didn't speak, again just staring at him, tears gleaming on her cheeks. Then a tension went out of her, as if she'd been relieved of a load she'd been carrying for far too long. 'I knew that,' she said. 'Or at least, I told myself I knew that. But there was always this doubt. And when you came and took me to safety, I didn't even look back. I just…left them there with no memorial, no one to remember them, no nothing.' She paused and swallowed. 'It feels wrong that I was the one who got to walk away. Do you…do you think I'm a coward for leaving?'

He stared down at her, conscious of a growing, ferocious need to soothe her, comfort her, reassure her, and he didn't question it. All he knew was that he'd do anything to ease her pain.

'No,' he said, letting her see the conviction

in his gaze. 'You're as far from a coward as it's possible to get. You survived for a week on your own in a very dangerous place. You were brave and stubborn and resourceful. You stayed with your family as long as you could, but in the end you had to leave. I think your parents would have been proud of you, and very glad that you found safety.' He ran his thumb along the side of her jaw in a feather-light caress. 'Also, while you might think that I rescued you, it was you who rescued me.'

She blinked. 'I rescued you?'

'From the darkness. From despair. You gave me hope, Elena, I told you that.' He let go of her chin and brushed away her tears. 'You saved me as much as I saved you.'

She searched his gaze for a long moment, though what she saw there, he had no idea. 'I'm glad I did, in that case,' she said hoarsely. 'I'm glad I was there. And, you know, I didn't totally leave them behind. My family, I mean. I kept some parts of them with me. The parts that make me happy. The good memories.' She paused. 'Do you have good memories of Dorian?'

The change of subject took him off guard and for a minute he couldn't think. Did he have good memories of Dorian? He'd avoided thinking of his brother for so long, he wasn't sure. 'I...' He stopped.

'No, go on,' Elena said. 'Tell me about him.'

He didn't want to revisit that particular agony, yet she'd told him about her family and her own painful doubts, and it seemed wrong not to give her something in return.

'He...was a rule follower,' Atticus began haltingly. 'But he could be persuaded to break the rules sometimes. He taught me how to sail in the sea around Kalifos and he taught me how to swim. When I stole cookies from the pantry and the housekeeper found out, he took the blame.' It was painful to think of him, exquisitely so, and yet...there was a sweetness to the memories that eased the pain. 'He told me ghost stories that terrified me so much I couldn't sleep, and he let me play with his toys when I was sick. He taught me how to fish...'

Elena's mouth had softened and it was curving in one of her beautiful smiles. 'He sounds like a good brother.'

'He was.' Atticus's voice was hoarse and he knew he should give her more, but all of a sudden he'd reached the end of what he could deal with right now. The combination of her loss and his own was too much, and he didn't want to talk any more. But she knew and she must have been feeling the same way, because abruptly she went up on her toes and pressed her mouth to his.

Desire leapt high and he was powerless to resist it. He didn't want to resist it. It was a fire that cauterised all wounds and he wanted to throw himself into the conflagration and let himself burn.

Clearly Elena was in agreement, because she got rid of her robe with a shrug of her shoulders, letting it slip to the ground. Then she was bare as she should always be with him, and his hands were on her hips, propelling her to the bed then taking her down onto it.

He pinned her beneath him, desperate for her, and she didn't deny him. She closed her legs around his waist, put her arms around his neck, kissing him hungrily. Then her hands stroked down his back, her hips lifting against his, encouraging him and so he sheathed himself in her welcoming heat.

He looked down at her as he began to

move, locked in the moment, all thoughts of the past fading, the ground glass in his heart loosening, the pleasure she gave him blunting the edges.

Her dark eyes were full of heat and yet beneath that heat lay something else, an emotion that burned hotter and fiercer, and he couldn't look away.

She had given him so many things he'd never had from anyone else. Understanding and sympathy. Kindness and comfort.

She's not just hope to you. She's something more.

But he didn't want to think about what more she was, not now, not with the ghosts of his brother and her family still in the room, so he pushed the thought away and lost himself in the darkness of her eyes and the heat of her body, until there was only her and the fire they created between them, and the rest of the world ceased to exist.

CHAPTER TEN

ELENA WOKE THE next morning to find herself wrapped around Atticus's hard, hot body. The sun was already shining through the big windows, the sea gleaming a deep blue through the glass.

He'd kept her up all night, taking her again and again as if he couldn't get enough of her, as if he were escaping his terrible past and all the pain that came with it by gorging himself on pleasure. She couldn't blame him. She'd felt the same way after she'd told him about her family and her doubts about how she'd left them. She'd thought she'd regret telling him and yet...

'You're as far from a coward as it's possible to get.'

There had been so much conviction in his eyes and in his voice that she couldn't help but think that maybe she'd been too hard on herself. Maybe she didn't have to listen to those doubts after all.

'You saved me.'

She shut her eyes, going back over the memory of his confession about his brother. She'd known all about that tragedy, but she hadn't known how deeply it still ate away at him. And it really wasn't any wonder. Atticus was a good man, a man with a deep need to care for people, and the accident that had taken his brother's life had scarred him deeply.

She'd known as she'd stood in front of him the night before and seen his gaze look through her, full of a horror that only he saw as he relived the moment of that terrible hunting accident. She hadn't meant for the conversation to take that turn, but he was the one who'd brought Dorian up, and then had told her all about what had happened that day.

No wonder he still felt the pain. He'd had the responsibility of his brother's death on his shoulders, the unbearable weight of it only made more unbearable by his father's blame too.

She could forgive Aristeidis many things, but she almost couldn't forgive him that. Except, Aristeidis's own regrets had eaten away at him, and he'd wanted to apologise to his son, so the intention had been there at least.

But she could see now why Atticus hadn't wanted anything to do with him.

Her heart still aching, she opened her eyes and shifted in his arms, turning to face him, expecting him to be asleep only to find his black eyes on hers.

'Good morning, Elenitsa,' he said in a sleep-roughened voice. 'I'm sorry, I kept you up far too late last night.'

'It's okay.' She searched his face, hoping she wouldn't see the pain that had been there last night, but his expression was clear. 'I'm sorry for last night too,' she went on impulsively. 'I shouldn't have got out of the bath so abruptly and left without talking to you. And I'm sorry you felt you had to explain what happened—'

'It's all right,' he said quietly. 'I wanted to tell you. I wanted you to know.'

Her heart twisted at the look in his eyes. 'Thank you for sharing the memories of Dorian with me.'

His mouth curved. 'It was good. I need to remember him more like that and less…' He stopped, but she didn't need him to elaborate, she knew what he meant. 'I would like to hear about your family,' he went on. 'Tell me your good memories of them.'

A little burst of surprise went through her. 'You really want to hear?'

'Of course.' He lifted a finger and brushed a curl from her forehead. 'Will you share them with me?'

She felt stupidly shy and yet she loved that he'd asked her. It had always been difficult to remember, because whenever she did, it was always accompanied by a dragging sense of shame. As if she didn't deserve to have even the good parts of her family. But that shame had lessened now, as if her confession to him the night before had drained the bulk of it away.

'Oh, it's just little things,' she said. 'Dad used to take me skating on the lake in winter and he'd lift me up in his arms, making me feel as if I was flying. And my mother used to make the best hot chocolate.' She smiled, remembering. 'I hated waking up in the mornings so she'd tell me that if I was a good girl and got up on time, there would be a mug of hot chocolate in the kitchen for me. And there always was.' They were small memories of little moments, and now, robbed of the shame, they were joyful and it felt good to share them with him. 'My little sister used to steal my toys and it would drive me crazy and I'd get so angry with her. But after we argued, she'd always throw her arms around my waist and beg me to forgive her.'

Atticus's dark gaze didn't move from hers. 'And you did?'

'Yes. Always.' A familiar bittersweet grief wound through her. 'We used to have the loudest family dinners and we'd argue with each other a lot, but we also laughed a lot too. My dad had the most ridiculous sense of humour, while my mother's was more sarcastic and sly.'

Atticus shifted against her, pulling her more firmly into his arms. 'And you're somewhere in the middle, I think. Though erring towards sarcastic.'

There was an amusement in his voice that almost sounded tender and it made her chest feel tight. 'How would you know?' she asked, realising as soon as she said it that it sounded more like an accusation than the joke she'd been meaning it as. 'I mean, you don't know me that well.'

His dark eyes held hers, the amusement fading from them. 'I know that you love swimming naked in the sea. I know that you don't like to talk when you're eating something delicious because you want to savour the taste. I know that you're quick to learn, and your mind and the way you think are fascinating to me. I know that you smell of apples and that when you come, you say my name.'

A flush crept over her. She hadn't known he'd been paying attention, that he'd been collecting pieces of her all this time. He'd called her his hope and she'd thought that was how he saw her, as an ideal, a cipher, not as a woman.

'I know that your anger is quick to rouse,' he went on. 'And yet you let it go just as quickly, and that your eyes are full of sparks when you're sharpening your claws on me. And I know that you're very strong and very stubborn and I find that maddening.'

She flushed deeper. 'Atticus…'

'Yet I also know that arguing with you is one of life's pleasures and that it excites me.

I know that you like trying new things, that you ask a lot of questions, and are very competitive. I know that in the evening, in the last rays of the sun, when you're lying on the sand, you look like you've been dipped in gold.'

Her throat closed and she couldn't speak.

'And I know that for some reason you're afraid of something,' he went on in the same quiet voice. 'And you won't tell me what it is or why.'

She looked away. 'I'm not afraid.'

'Yes, you are,' he said, quietly insistent. 'You were afraid last night, that's why you got out of the bath.'

Elena lifted her hands and pushed against his chest, needing some space. Because of course she was afraid, she just didn't want to explain it to him, when she barely knew herself what was making her so afraid. Only that it had something to do with wanting more from him, wanting something she knew she was never going to have.

And you know all about that, don't you?

That was why she tried to remember only the good parts of the time she had with her family, the parts that didn't hurt. Not the terrible ache of grief that had never left her, the wanting of something she would never have.

Atticus let her push him away, not making any move as she sat on the side of the bed, catching the sheet protectively around her, needing the distance.

All those things he'd said about her, all those things he'd noticed… They were all her, all parts of herself that Aristeidis had never seen, because for him, she suspected, she'd always been a sign that his son wasn't completely gone from him. A second chance he hadn't thought he'd have, and while those weren't bad things, they weren't entirely about her, either.

But Atticus had noticed them. Atticus had seen deeper into her, and it made her feel vulnerable.

'I'm fine.' She forced out the words. 'There really wasn't anything—'

But she didn't get to finish, because Atticus abruptly grabbed her and she found herself hauled back and pinned beneath him on the bed once again.

She put up a cursory resistance, but then he took her wrists and pinned them to the mattress on either side of her head.

'No,' he said flatly, his black gaze burning into hers. 'You're not doing the equivalent of walking out on me, not again. Not after last night. Tell me what's bothering you and tell me now.'

Oh, she wished she didn't like it when he got insistent like this, when he held her so she couldn't escape. When he made it obvious that he wouldn't let her avoid his questions, because he wanted to know. Because she mattered to him.

She wished she had the willpower to shove him away. It would be so much easier than having to tell him the truth.

And what is the truth?

Her mouth dried. 'It's stupid. I just... wanted to be more than a cipher to you. I wanted...'

'What? What do you want?'

Love. You want him to love you.

The thought struck her like a bullet from a gun, a direct hit, and for a moment she couldn't breathe. She'd asked him at the reading of Aristeidis's will whether love came into any of this and he'd looked at her with his fierce black gaze and had said love had nothing to do with it.

That had been her first warning, and she hadn't listened. She'd thought that sleeping with him, that a wedding and a honeymoon, wouldn't impact her intentions not to let him get under her skin. She'd thought she was strong, that she could hold out against him, and yet…

He was a combination of arrogance, fierce primal beauty, along with a protectiveness, a gentleness and a kindness she hadn't expected. And last night he'd shown her that there was a vulnerability to him too that had crept under her defences and laid waste to her heart. The tragedy that shaped him, that ate away at him, that had propelled him to create his charity that changed the lives of so many people in the entire world… That took drive and focus, and ambition, but fundamentally it took a deep caring for people and a need to help them, and that was what he had in abundance.

She'd been silly to think she could hold out against him, that he wouldn't change her just as deeply as she'd changed him. Silly to think that she could forget the deep sense of trust she'd felt the moment he'd seen her in the rubble and had saved her. Had altered the course of her life for ever.

Except how could she tell him that? When love was the one thing he'd told her very firmly was out of the question?

And why would he love you anyway? No one stays. Everyone leaves you in the end.

'Elena.' Atticus was frowning now as he studied her. 'What is it?'

Her sense of vulnerability deepened and she really did want to pull away then, but his grip on her wrists was too strong and the weight of him pinning her too great for her to shift. She was surrounded by his heat and his sunshine and salt scent, and the feel of his body on hers… He made her feel safe and yet threatened at the same time.

'Elena,' he insisted.

And she knew that there was no escape. That she'd have to tell him. And that once she had, everything would change. She would lose him the way she lost everyone else who'd ever mattered to her.

'I love you,' she burst out. 'That's what the problem is. I love you and I can't think of anything better than living with you as your wife. Of creating the future we both wanted, with children, having a family. But a family to me means love, Atticus, and if we don't have that between us...' Her throat closed, but she forced the words out. 'I don't want to be your hope. I want to be your love.'

At first Atticus wasn't quite sure what she'd said. And then, as he stared down into her dark eyes, seeing the fear in them along with her usual fierce stubbornness, the words finally penetrated.

She loved him.

She *loved* him.

It felt as if something had grabbed him hard by the throat and refused to let go.

Love wasn't supposed to be a part of this, it was *never* supposed to be a part of this. He didn't want it. Love was the horror of seeing your brother dead on the ground and knowing it was because of you, and that your life would never be the same again. Love was the anger in your father's eyes, and the blame too. Love turned to hate in the blink of an eye. Love wanted revenge.

He never wanted anything to do with it again, not even from her.

He let go of her and pushed himself off the bed.

Elena sat up, her hair cascading around her head in a long golden fall. Wrapped in the white sheet, her pale shoulders revealed, she looked heartbreakingly beautiful and so fragile he wanted to wrap her up and hide her away so no one could ever hurt her.

Someone like you, perhaps?

He was already cold and that thought made him go even colder. She couldn't love him, it was impossible. One day he'd make a mistake, do something unforgivable, and that love would turn to hate. That love would destroy what relationship they'd managed to build and he couldn't allow that to happen. He just couldn't.

'No,' he said flatly. 'I'm sorry, Elena, but no.'

'What do you mean no?'

'I told you. Love can't be part of this. Not at all.'

Her chin lifted, her backbone straightening. 'Well, that's too bad, isn't it? Because I love you.'

He found himself shaking his head. 'Why? What on earth about me is there to love?'

She just stared at him. 'Didn't you hear yourself saying all those things you noticed about me? All those things you know about me that no one else ever has. You…you make me feel good, Atticus.'

He gave a bitter laugh. 'That's just the sex talking.'

Anger flickered in her eyes. 'No, it's not. I might be inexperienced but I know the difference between sexual obsession and love.' Her gaze focused abruptly on him. 'Do you?'

Of course he knew. Did she think he'd never felt love before? 'I know what love is,' he spat. 'It's the horror of finding out you killed the person who was most important to you in the whole world. It's the hate in your father's eyes whenever he looks at you. It's having the people you care about slam doors in your face and cut you off without recourse and all because you made a mistake. One simple mistake.' He was breathing very fast now, all his muscles tense, the pressure inside him building and building. 'I don't want anything to do with love ever again.'

There was a long moment of silence where he was conscious of his harsh, ragged breathing, as if he'd run a long race. Then Elena slid off the bed, leaving the sheet behind her and coming over to him. She was naked, her body all soft pink and cream curves. The look in her eyes was soft and that terrible understanding was back, as if she knew his pain. As if she'd experienced it herself.

She stopped in front of him, her expression full of a fierce tenderness. 'I won't do that to you, Atticus,' she said. 'I won't ever do that to you.'

But he was shaking his head, his heartbeat loud in his ears. 'You don't know that. Aristeidis, I'm sure, thought he would never do that too, and then I killed Dorian and all that love he had for me was gone. It didn't matter that I was his son, Elena. Love didn't matter at all.'

Her eyes were very dark, tenderness burning in them like a flame. 'I can see why you'd think that,' she said. 'Believe me, I can see. But don't you think it can be different with us?'

'No, I don't. And why would I ever take that chance anyway?' He wanted to touch her very badly, but he knew that would be a bad idea, so he kept his hands to himself. 'I could hurt you, Elena. I could…hurt any children we have. And that…would destroy me.'

Her gaze turned liquid, tears glittering in her eyes, but she didn't look away, her expression still fierce.

They made everything worse, those tears. They made that ground-glass feeling in his heart return, a burning agony that he could never outrun.

'You won't do that though,' she said passionately. 'You won't. You're the most caring, the most protective, the most gentle man I've ever known. You saved me all those years ago, Atticus. You brought me home to your father. You gave me a life I'd never thought I'd have. And you'd never hurt me, you'd never hurt our family either.'

He searched her beautiful face. 'But aren't I? Aren't I hurting you right now?'

She didn't look away, the vulnerability in her eyes so painful it made him catch his breath. She was always so strong and so determined, but he could see the need in her. For him. 'Yes,' she admitted.

'It'll pass,' he ground out. 'Give it time.'

But she shook her head. 'I never wanted to need anyone. I never wanted to be vulnerable, not after the earthquake. Not after I lost my family. Then you came and you made me feel safe for the first time since my family died, and I thought… I thought I could trust you. But then you took me to Kalifos and you left me there, and I felt abandoned. So I decided that day that I wasn't going to ever need you again.'

Her voice thickened even more, but the burning look in her eyes didn't waver. 'But I do, Atticus, I need you. I always have, right from that moment you saw me in the rubble. And I think I always will.'

He remembered that moment. When he'd left her with the housekeeper on Kalifos and there had been tears streaming down her face. 'Don't go,' she'd whispered in the Greek she was already getting very good at. 'Please don't leave me here.'

But he'd had to and he couldn't stay. That was when he'd had to harden his heart, to detach himself from his emotions.

He had to do that now, because he'd made a mistake, he could see that so clearly now. Yet another mistake. He'd let her mean something to him. He'd let her matter and now he was hurting her. He'd never wanted to hurt her.

'I'm sorry,' he said, and he meant it. 'But this is something I can't do. Love can't be part of our marriage, Elena, and that's final.'

For a moment, she stared at him. Then abruptly she took a step closer, all pink and golden nakedness, and she went on her toes and pressed a kiss to his mouth. But it was so brief, so achingly brief, and he knew it was a goodbye.

'Then I'm sorry,' she said, her gaze ferocious. 'But I can't do a marriage without love.'

And before he could say a word, she walked past him and out of the bedroom.

CHAPTER ELEVEN

ELENA CALLED THE Kalathes staff and organised a helicopter to come to the island. Atticus didn't follow her. After she'd arranged her transport, she went back to the bedroom to tell him she was leaving, but he wasn't there.

Her heart felt as if it were shattering in her chest, but she ignored the pain as she went around the room, packing up her belongings, tears running down her cheeks.

She let them fall. It didn't matter if she cried and it felt cathartic. Even her tears hadn't been enough to make him stay, even baring her heart. He was right after all, love didn't matter. Perhaps it never had.

Then again, why she thought it would, she had no idea. She should never have told him how she felt, but he'd demanded the truth from her and so she'd given it to him. Then when

she'd said it and when he'd recoiled, she'd felt
the oddest sense of calm wash over her.

He couldn't do this—she knew he
wouldn't—and even her honesty, even her
tears, even her anger and her passion weren't
enough. But the pain in her heart was sweet
despite it all. The love she felt for him, a
bright glow, a ball of sunshine that she knew
would never dim. She could feel its strength,
its peace. It wasn't a weakness at all, and yes,
there was pain, but the feeling itself was calm
and strong and right as a heartbeat.

If ever there was a man who needed love
in his life, it was Atticus Kalathes. And while
he might not accept it, she wasn't going to
deny loving him. And she wasn't going to
stop. She would just have to love him in other
ways, from afar, and it would have to be from
afar. While she might love him, she wasn't
going to compromise on what she needed,
not this time.

He was in agony, she could see that, but
she couldn't deny what was in her own heart.
It was dishonest. She couldn't bring her children into a world with a father who thought
love was destructive, who didn't want anything to do with it. She couldn't create a

family without it. She remembered her own family, those bright moments of joy that she kept close to her heart, and in every single one of them was evidence of love. Evidence of the caring they'd had for each other.

She wanted that again. She wanted it desperately. She'd tried to have it on Kalifos with Aristeidis, but it had been so one-sided. She, giving everything to Aristeidis, while he had been so caught up in his own grief he hadn't noticed.

She couldn't do that with Atticus, not again.

Perhaps it was cutting off her nose to spite her face, but if that was the case then so be it. She couldn't build a life and a family with a man who didn't love her. She wouldn't.

Tears dripped slowly down her face as she doggedly finished packing and then got dressed in simple jeans and a T-shirt. The clothing felt rough and uncomfortable after the days of having nothing on her bare skin but sun, yet she ignored the discomfort just as she ignored everything else.

Once she was packed, she debated trying to find Atticus to tell him where she'd gone, and then decided not to. He'd deliberately taken himself away from her and there wasn't any benefit to going after him. He'd see the helicopter when it landed and know she was leaving anyway.

Her heart aching, Elena picked up her bag and walked out of the house to the jetty to wait.

Atticus watched her from the other end of the beach, a small figure sitting hunched over on the jetty, her hair blowing around like a golden flag in the breeze that came off the sea.

Every part of him was in agony. He'd tried very hard to detach himself, running hard along the beach, hoping physical exercise would help him find that space where he could be free of the pain. Where his focus would subsume everything, the past lost in the moment of the present.

But he couldn't lose himself. All he could see was Elena's pale face and the fierce light in her eyes. All he could hear was her voice telling him how much she needed him.

How can you let her leave?

He had to, that was the issue. He couldn't insist she stay. She wanted something from him that he didn't want to give, and it was too much. He couldn't ask her not to love him and he couldn't keep on insisting on a marriage that wouldn't give her what she needed.

He wasn't that man.

If she wanted to leave, he had to let her go.

If you let go of her, you let go of hope.

He sat on the rocks, ignoring the sting of rough granite against his bare flesh, watching her. He'd called her his hope, but she'd wanted to be more than just an ideal, more than a talisman, and she was.

Over the past couple of weeks she'd become so much more. Warmth and comfort and a source of strength. Understanding and sympathy. And laughter. Joy. So many things he'd never thought he'd find again until she came into his life. All the things that were intrinsic to her, and weren't merely a representation in platinum. A child reaching up their arms.

She wasn't a child. She was a grown woman, with thoughts and feelings and dreams of her own, and she had to be free to live them. He couldn't keep hold of her just because of what she'd once represented to him.

If she's more than that to you, why are you giving her up?

He shook his head, trying to get rid of the voice inside him. But it wouldn't go away. He *had* to give her up. He couldn't, wouldn't have anything to do with love again.

If you give her up, you also give up all the good things that came with it. The joy, the happiness, the comfort, the strength...

His jaw was tight, his shoulders tighter. He tore his gaze from the jetty where she sat, hoping if he didn't see her, he wouldn't remember his arms around her, her laugh in his ears, the smiles she gave him. The peace in his heart when she was in his arms. The comfort of her touch...

'*Do you have good memories of Dorian?*' she'd asked.

And he had remembered. So many good things that had been lost under his grief and his pain.

Love is pain, but it's also all those other things too. Comfort and joy and happiness. Love is charity too.

Atticus shut his eyes. His charity was a business and he ran it as such. He'd wanted to give people hope.

Where do you think hope comes from?

A strange feeling coiled inside him, a powerful intensity that he didn't understand. Hope came from…well, it came from a little girl in the rubble. It came from finding a moment of brightness in the midst of the darkness. It came from…

It comes from love.

Atticus took a breath and another, the feeling like a pressure starting to burst. He'd loved his brother and he'd loved his father, and there had been good things in those relationships. It hadn't all been horror and pain and grief.

She found happiness in the midst of despair. Why can't you? She showed you the way. All you have to do is follow her.

Every part of him felt as if he were going to burst apart. Was it that simple? Could he just accept the pain, the agony, the horror again?

You already have. And it's as simple as picking up a little girl in the rubble.

He couldn't breathe. Could he do this? Could he accept what she wanted, what she demanded? Could he open himself up to what he'd been avoiding all these years?

Except…he'd never avoided it, had he? All

that feeling he was trying to deny, all the pain and grief, were locked up tight in his heart. But all the joy and the happiness were locked up there too.

You can't have one without the other. But it's easier to have the pain when she's around to help you bear it.

It came to him, in a bolt from the blue, that he'd spent years detaching himself. Years telling himself he felt nothing, distracting himself from the storm inside him. But he hadn't distracted himself. He'd started a charity, for God's sake. And it wasn't because he felt nothing. It was because he felt *everything*.

It rushed through him then, the pain and the agony, but also the joy, the happiness. The bright moments that Elena had talked about, and treasured. Her beneath him, her eyes full of desire. Her laughing as he tickled her foot. Her face flushed with pleasure as she held up a fish she'd caught...

He couldn't have one without the other, and he realised all of a sudden that he didn't want to. She embraced both parts of love and so could he.

Where she led, he would follow. He had to. He couldn't do anything else.

He shoved himself off the rocks and ran hard across the beach, across the hot sand to the path to the jetty and then down it.

She lifted her head as he approached then stood up. 'The helicopter is coming,' she began.

'I'm cancelling the helicopter,' he said.

She blinked then glanced behind her as if she wanted to back away, but there was only the sea behind her. He didn't stop coming.

'Atticus,' she said, but then he was right in front of her and this time it was he who lifted his arms to her, putting them around her and sweeping her up in them, holding her where she was always meant to be. Against his chest, against his heart.

She pushed against him once then stopped, going lax as if she was too tired to struggle any more. A tear slid down her nose, her dark eyes full of pain. 'What are you doing? I told you I couldn't—'

'I know what you told me.' He looked down at her, seeing how she hurt and knowing it was his fault, but also knowing that he was going to spend the rest of his life healing that hurt. 'But I was wrong. So I changed my mind. Or rather, you helped me change it.

You made me see that love doesn't have to be destructive. That it's not only about pain and grief, but also about happiness and joy and I… I want that. I want more of that. I want you to teach me more, show me more. More happiness. More joy. More laughter. I want bright moments and precious memories, and I want to create them with you. I want memories we can treasure for the rest our lives, because…' His heart thundered in his head and the only thing that was real was her lying in his arms. 'I love you, Elenitsa. It feels as if I've loved you for ever.'

Her mouth had opened in shock, her eyes going wide. She searched his face as if looking for the truth and he made sure she saw it. He let her see all the love in his heart that he'd denied for too many years. He let it out.

'Oh, Atticus…' There were more tears in her eyes, but they weren't of sadness, not this time. 'I just…want happiness for you more than anything in the whole world.'

'Then let's find it,' he said. 'Let's find it together.'

'Are you sure?' she whispered. 'Are you sure this is what you want?'

'I'm sure.' And he could feel the certainty

settled down inside him, and he already knew that this would be one of those bright moments, a precious memory that he would look at later in life and treasure for ever. 'You're not my hope after all, Elena. All this time, you were my love.'

She reached up to him then, and put her arms around him, and her mouth was on his and there was so much warmth and sweetness in her kiss that he wondered how he could ever have walked away from her.

Well, he wasn't going to any more. He never would again.

He turned with her in his arms, and he carried her back to the house, and together they started making those moments, moments full of happiness, moments full of joy. Moments full of love, that would last them the rest of their lives.

EPILOGUE

ATTICUS THREW THE wreath Elena had made out of wildflowers into the sea, and then pulled her in close to his side. She held their son in her arms, his dark head on her shoulder. Dorian Aristeidis Kalathes was quiet now, but he'd proved himself to be a handful right from the moment of his birth.

Atticus wouldn't have it any other way.

The wreath was for his father, the first anniversary of Aristeidis's death, and it had been Elena's idea to mark the occasion with flowers cast on the sea and then, like counting a rosary, he would remember the good moments, the treasured moments that Atticus had of his father, and of Dorian.

He spoke the words now without faltering, the pain bittersweet yet bearable, because there had been some good moments. Some very good moments. Moments he wanted to remember so he could rebuild the relationship between them that had been broken. His father wasn't around to help, but Atticus couldn't help feeling that somehow, wherever he was, Aristeidis knew and approved.

He had a feeling that Aristeidis would approve of the little family he and Elena had created for themselves over the past year too. They'd set about incorporating parts of Kalathes Shipping into Eleos, making their own shipping network that greatly facilitated delivery of important supplies to various needy countries around the world. Elena was a proven genius when it came to logistics and supply-chain issues, and she'd already improved some of Eleos's operations immeasurably.

She'd improved his life immeasurably, too, bringing to it a lightness and joy he'd never experienced before. A happiness he'd never thought he'd have.

The wreath drifted over the water, two seabirds hovering over it, their wings motionless in the air. Then they flew into the sky, circling Atticus and Elena and their son once before disappearing.

'I think he and Dorian liked our gesture,'

Elena murmured as they watched the birds disappear into the sky.

Atticus hadn't ever believed in signs or portents. He'd never believed in fate. And once, he hadn't believed in love.

But he was different now. He'd changed. And now, he believed.

He believed in love with every beat of his heart.

'I think they did,' he said, his heart finally free of the chains of guilt and grief and bitterness.

Then he put his arm around his wife and his son, and they all went back to the villa. Ready to create yet more memories, yet more moments of joy, a never-ending chain that would last them all the days of their lives.

* * * * *